SEDUCING Amelia

SEDUCING AMELIA

Plump Playwright Act II

As a librarian, curvy Amelia is determined to drag this town out of its illiterate rating, no matter the reader's preferences. So, when sweet elderly Maude asks for something with a little steam in it, Amy doesn't hesitate to recommend her own erotic novels. She'd written them on a lark, and eleven books into the Masculine Manipulation series, her nom de plume is a household name.

When Maude's 'charming' grandson, Tom Bradshaw, storms into Amy's idyllic life, she learns that the men in her books pale in comparison. Sure, Tom's gorgeous and intelligent with lips she could sculpt in clay, but he's also an opinionated ass who can't seem to leave her alone.

Especially now that he's read her novels.

Also by Sevannah Storm

The Blood of Legends Series

The Huntress

The Healer

*

The Gifting Series

Soul Forged

Fate Forged

Sun Forged

War Forged

Star Forged

Shadow Forged

Earth Forged

Lust Forged

Fire Forged

*

The Qaldreth Warriors

Sol Survivor

Dark Survivor (Coming soon)

*

The Space Hunter Chronicles

The Shikari

The Justisaar

*

Inkounter Series

Inkoded

*

Standalones

Xiaxan Fox

Ire of Silver

The Crucible of the Eternal

*

Plump Playwright Series

Plump Jane

Seducing Amelia

Loving Finley

Keeping Tessa

Kissing Navy

Chapter One

Silence descended on Amelia's small world when the front door of the library clicked shut. Sonja had, at last, gone home for the day, leaving Amy alone in the quiet, book-scented library. The setting sun offered a final illusion of warmth through the windows high above the shelves.

Ambling to the record player to the rear of the building, she paused to tidy books before slipping a vinyl record out of its sleeve. She placed it on the turntable with a reverent touch, lifted the needle with a steady finger, then lowered it.

Pavarotti's Viva La Traviata Le Brindisi filled the small confines of the quaint library. She closed her eyes, raised her face to the ceiling, and allowed his dulcet voice to soothe her. She shivered, wishing she knew a man with such a deep tenor. Her nipples hardened under her vintage button-up blouse at the imagery alone.

She stored that feeling, having assessed it from all angles for her writing. Whatever lost desire, love, and longing she experienced, she poured into her novels. Then before she fell asleep, whatever lingered, she'd take care of like she attended to her anti-aging rituals.

In tiny Gainsford, she was spinster at twenty-eight with no prospects other than Phillipe Lorenzo, her neighbor's son, who insisted on treating her to dinner when he visited from the 'big city.' He tried every time for a little affection, but no, dinner didn't equal sex in her mind, no matter how much she longed for someone to love her.

Balancing a stack of books against her ample bosom, she navigated the shelves, waltzing, and sashaying down the aisles. She hummed or sang along, pausing only to replay it. As crisp as the digital version was, it couldn't compare to the authenticity of an LP.

To slide in a book at the base of the shelf, she had to bend at the waist and balance on her platform pumps—a weakness of hers. She hadn't seen the man enter the library or approach her, just sensed his shadow when it was too late. With a yelp, she bolted upright, leaped back, bounced off a bookshelf, and teetered on her heels for a moment before slumping to the floor.

"What the f...physics 530 do you think you are doing?" She huffed her hair out of her face to glare at the intruder.

Her breath hitched, and she blinked. The fashion for criminals must have changed. Since when did they wear crisp gray suits that molded to broad shoulders and bulging biceps? He was too tanned, as if he'd just returned from a tropical island. Which was possible if he was the head of a drug cartel. Now, that made sense.

One moment she sprawled before him like a ritual offering, the next, she was in his arms, his hands gripping her waist. His navy-blue shirt gaped, tuffs of ebony hair peeked through. His cologne overpowered the musty library, citrus and grass... Delicious. He waited as if to ensure she wouldn't fall over, then with a curt nod, released her.

"My apologies..."

Whatever he said after that, she couldn't say. Holy Dostoyevsky, his voice rumbled like distant thunder. Her calmed nipples tightened, and tingles spread across her breasts. Wow, she had no words to describe the sensation. It couldn't be instant attraction. Sure, she wrote about it, but was this proof of its existence or an urban legend?

His cheeks darkened, and he clenched his jaw, waiting for her to speak.

Blinking at him, as if dazed, she opened her mouth, but her mind wouldn't fire a thought.

"Listen, I don't have time for this bullshit. I'd like the contact details for Ms. Amelia Perkins."

She frowned. Why did he want to speak to her? In that harsh tone, she wouldn't be helpful, not when he'd scared her to death then hummed desire through her body. Here in Gainsford, a man had to buy a woman dinner, then kiss her, among other intimacies, to get her to this stage of readiness. This man just had to use that lethal voice of his.

She narrowed her eyes. "We don't give out staff information. You can leave a message with me, and I'll let her know."

His arched brow looked like a crow's wing. "Are you the head librarian?"

"Sometimes." She wanted to snort, to roll her eyes, but ladies never acted in such a vulgar manner, or so her mother claimed. Little did she know of Amy's other proclivities.

The phone rang—Sonja's goodnight call. Amy darted around the man, ignoring his looming physique, tantalizing cologne, and glower. She launched herself across the check-in desk and grabbed the phone.

"Sonja, you're home?"

"Why are you breathless?" Sonja sounded too eager and suspicious for Amy's liking. If she hinted she wasn't alone, ever-romantic Sonja would rush over to matchmake.

"Had to run for the phone." If she hadn't answered, Sonja would return to the library, and there went Amy's blissful evening.

She glanced at the man, watching him approach her. Long strides, pinched lips, and intense focus made for one hell of a brooding package. She clenched her thighs together against the rush of heat, which was a struggle when she had one foot on the floor and the other hovering mid-air.

"All right, have a lovely evening, and don't work too late." Sonja clicked off.

Amy returned the phone to the cradle, her secret life curling her lips into a delicious smile. Sonja thought Amy worked all hours at the library. Little did she know about her novels. She raised her gaze to rest on Sonja's pixie-haired she-devil photo mounted on the wall right below Amy's with the hold plaque announcing her title as Head Librarian.

Dammit. She spun on her foot, lowered the other, and sidled in front of the framed staff photographs. Too late.

"Right, Ms. Perkins, let's discuss your book selection." He folded his arms across his chest, and he seemed to grow in stature. An ebony curl fell across his temple as he narrowed his hazel eyes.

She gasped. "What? Why?" She had an extensive selection and had worked hard to make the right choices for her small town. Today, two teenagers she'd never seen before requested library cards.

He yanked a familiar book out of his jacket pocket, struggling with it for a bit. His massive hands must have wedged it in there. A semi-nude couple in a passionate embrace splashed across the cover. A black leather bustier hinted at something more than missionary style. Gemma James was the author, and that would be Amelia Perkins if one looked at her taxes.

He slammed the book onto the check-in counter, his fingers an inch from her hip. "This filth should not be in my grandmother's hands. What were you thinking?"

Filth? Fury pulsed her heartbeat behind her left eye, and she settled her hands on her hips. How dare he? "Have you read it?"

Horror contorted his handsome features. "I don't have time to read drivel, Ms. Perkins."

Wait. Grandmother? The only elderly woman who'd checked this book out was Maude.

She tapped her bottom lip with a fingertip and circled him, running a critical yet admiring gaze over his body. Her fingers itched to peel his jacket off. With those biceps, he had to have a matching backside, tight enough to bounce quarters off.

"Mm, let me guess, you're a discontented accountant, an unfulfilled banker, some hot-shot litigator, or an egotistical executive with no appreciation for literature." It didn't matter what he did during the day, images of him making her scream shot heat to her extremities.

He growled and stepped closer, casting shadows across all her exits.

"Too close for comfort? Oh, dear me. Well, let me explain it in terms you'll understand. Banging the same type of woman for say fifty years, wouldn't that grow tiresome, *sir*?" She scooped her book off the counter and ran a caressing finger across its edges, as if to apologize for the Neanderthal's abuse. Forbidden Nights had been her first, and yes, she'd come far since then. "The same applies to reading. Some people can handle repeated, meaningless sessions, but sweet Maude asked for something steamier."

"My grandmother is—"

"Tired of the same-old regency stories she's read since she was a young girl." Amy sighed, boredom tapping her foot. She wanted a roaring fire, a glass of sherry, and her laptop. "Listen, Mr. Banker, if you think for one moment I didn't try and talk Maude out of her choice, then you're an idiot. Contrary to your belief, she's a grown woman, stubborn, opinionated, and quite eloquent. Now, had she been underage, she wouldn't have left the library with anything this raunchy." Amy thumped the book against his chest. "Read it, and form an educated opinion."

She scooped another stack of books and sashayed away, restarting Pavarotti as she meandered along the aisles. Her dismissal was all a pretense. Every one of her senses and ounce of energy in her cells focused on him. He hesitated, glared, huffed, then stormed out, slamming the door behind him.

Holy Whitman, he was gorgeous. As she hummed, an idea formed. Perhaps she should immortalize him in her Masculine Manipulation series, book twelve? She chuckled; she'd make it the dirtiest of the dozen.

Chapter Two

THE FURY THAT HAD driven Tom from the Springs Retirement Village to the local library fizzled the moment he slammed the car door. His mind reeled, and a fine sweat had formed on his upper lip.

What the fuck just happened?

Librarians shouldn't look like that, not in his world. Her demure blouse, buttoned to her throat, molded to her breasts, and cinched in at her waist. Her calf-length skirt hugged her wide hips and thick thighs. He wasn't into plump women, but fuck, he would do her on the check-in counter, over her returns trolley, and against a bookshelf. Dark auburn hair curled against alabaster skin and with those bold ruby lips?

Her fragrance still lingered, something elusive, with hints of exotic flowers and waterfalls. As he adjusted his erection in his slacks, he stared at the book on the passenger seat. He'd gone there to have Gram's choice of material censored. What he hadn't expected was to have his attempts thwarted, his perceptions challenged.

He was Tom Bradshaw, the top attorney at Gibson, Smythe, and Bradshaw. No one gainsaid him or challenged him without having their ducks in a row. Yet this stunning woman had him on the back foot from the moment she'd fallen at his feet. She listened to opera, preferred not to swear, dressed like a 1950's pinup girl, and had the sensuality of his last ten lovers combined.

She'd been right about his choice of casual partners, a string of blonde women who seemed to pale against her vibrancy. He'd like nothing more than her lips wrapped around his cock.

Fuck.

He snatched the book, his hand trembling. Switching on the light, he flicked to the opening paragraph, expecting some bullshit romanticized approach to sex or something too gritty for his grandmother.

Two chapters later, he grunted and snapped the book closed, tossing it onto the seat again. Dammit, he'd enjoyed the introduction of the strong female heroine, her thoughts and reactions.

Rubbing the nape of his neck, he started the engine but didn't pull out of the parking lot. Something compelled him to ask Amelia Perkins to dinner. He clenched his jaw. The blondes she mentioned kept his baser urges satiated since he didn't have time to date.

Watching via the rearview mirror, the library's door opened, and Amelia stepped out. Bathed in the outside light, her hair warmed, and skin glowed. She sashayed down the sidewalk in those sexy shoes, her hips swaying. She looked lost in thought. He memorized her face before darkness consumed her.

She was alone on an empty street. Not liking her disregard for personal safety, he scowled. But he hesitated. Should he leap out to walk her home or drive behind her like a stalker?

After slamming his palms on the steering wheel, he switched off the engine, and climbed out. "Ms. Perkins?"

She stilled, then spun on a heel to tilt her head, a welcoming smile on those beguiling lips. When she saw him, it faltered, and she squared her shoulders. Said action thrust her breasts out. Her hard nipples tenting her blouse skittered his heart rate and dried his mouth.

He sighed, snapped the car door shut, and jogged to her. "Let me see you home."

"That's sweet of you to offer, Maude's grandson, but this is a small town, and I am perfectly safe. Good night." Her dark eyes sucked him in, and he stared into her upturned gaze.

He envisioned gripping her chin and descending his lips at a snail's pace as he admired her smooth complexion, the flutter of her eyelashes against her cheeks, and the sweet temptation of her lips. Kissing her would be beyond his most erotic dreams.

"It's Tom Bradshaw." Was that his voice, all hoarse and gravel-lined?

She nodded and turned.

He threw out a hand to capture her wrist. Her soft skin was so enticing, and her warmth called to him. He shifted closer. "Please, if Gram found out I didn't escort you… She can still box my ears."

Amelia laughed, sealing her fate with that throaty sound, the way it wrapped around his chest, his core. "I won't tell if you don't. It will be our secret." Her bright smile in the dim streetlight shot lightning to his groin, like spasms or shards of sharp pleasure. "Good night, Tom Bradshaw."

She curled her wrist out of his hand and walked away, not once glancing back.

He didn't know how long he stared after her, rocking on his toes as if his body needed him to follow her, to not lose her.

Cursing, he strode to his car, sliding into the driver's leather seat. He hit speed dial on his dashboard.

"Cal?" He cleared his throat and tried again now that he had his managing partner, Callum Gibson, on the line. "I need a few days." Tom paused. What was he doing? He never took a vacation.

"Is everything all right?" Cal's concern echoed his own. This was out of character for Tom, but fuck it. He needed to pursue this, even if it ended after one night. Well, one long night of mindless passion.

His balls spasmed, and he sighed. "Yes, Gram is well, I—"

"Take as long as you need. You have months of unclaimed vacation days." Cal's voice was muffled as if he held his phone to his ear between shoulder and chin. "She better be worth it, Tom."

Tom's mouth dried at the mere memory of Amelia. "She bowled me over, didn't cower when I glared at her, and just walked away from me as if I meant nothing to her."

"Whoa, challenge accepted." Cal laughed. "I don't need the details, not with Chrissy eavesdropping." Denials in the backdrop confirmed that his five-month pregnant wife was listening in. "I rest my case."

"Thanks, Cal. Kisses for my favorite lady." The one woman who might have stolen his heart now belonged to his best friend and partner.

"Sure, she'll have kisses…mine." Cal's tone were teasing, but his words were far from it.

Time to change the subject since he suspected Cal had known of Tom's earlier feelings for his wife. "I'll call in a few days. If all goes well, you'll see me sooner."

"Confidence isn't always attractive. Maybe try something else this time." Cal's advice might be correct in this instance, but Tom didn't want to discuss Amelia with him.

"When has my confidence failed me?" It had with Chrissy. He'd pursued her first, but she'd taken one look at Cal, and now, they were so happy, it was nauseating.

Cal sighed. "Chrissy wants to know one thing about this mystery woman."

"She doesn't like to swear." Tom smiled. Physics 530? Was that in the Dewey system?

"So, out of your league then?" Cal yelped, whispered something to Chrissy, and with a hurried goodbye, hung up.

Out of his league? Maybe Amelia was, but that wouldn't stop him from trying, not with the way his body throbbed. Fuck, he had no luggage and had made no reservations.

He'd drive the ninety minutes to his city apartment in Anham, pack and book a room at the local bed and breakfast, then return in the morning. It would give him plenty of time to rethink this madness. After all, he never exerted this much effort on any woman.

Would Amelia Perkins be worth it?

Chapter Three

AMY SHIVERED, UNLOCKED HER front door, and stepped into her duplex. Her body hummed, making demands she couldn't quite satiate. A single woman didn't have many choices when it came to sexual release unless she used the battery-powered kind. She debated whether to bath and ease the tension within her, thanks to a certain man, or channel it into her writing.

She toed off her pumps, dumped her handbag on the chair in the foyer, stripped her gloves off, and dropped them on top. A few steps into her quaint kitchen, she had the bottle and a sherry glass on the wooden counter. She threw back one glass of sherry, pausing to enjoy the sweet burn as it settled into her belly. With the glass and bottle in hand, she crossed her unused living room and entered the enclosed patio. The glass conservatory was warm in winter and cool in summer, providing heavenly views when she wrote.

With a hum of appreciation, she admired the starlit sky. When the breeze turned cold, she entered her house and slid the door shut. Refilling her glass, she settled behind the antique mahogany desk. She flipped open her laptop, waited a moment for it to boot up, then let her fingers fly across the keys.

The more she wrote, the more flustered she became, and the harder she punched the keyboard. She had sexual tension between the characters from the first chapter, with them doing it by the third. Sighing, she slumped in her chair, allowing her posture to relax for a moment. Then she stiffened, closed the document, and opened another. After another downed glass, she wrote the first chapter of Loving Finley.

Fin thought her life was perfect as a pediatric nurse who was madly in love with the resident surgeon. But when love turns to pain, she flees to her home, to work as a mountain guide, escorting groups of men through the mountains on a 'get-in-touch-with-their-inner-man' camp. She can handle herself and anything her mountain can throw at her. Except this. A flash flood strands her with the most gorgeous man on the planet.

Duke Delaney, some hotshot baseball star she's never heard of. He's handsome and he knows it. But falling in love isn't on her agenda. Hell, no, not happening. Now, she has to get Duke's sexy-as-sin ass to Old Margot's cabin and hope the radio's working.

By the time they'd reached the stashed emergency supplies, the sexual tension was off the charts. Growling, Amy slammed her laptop shut. Three hours she'd wasted, with thoughts of Tom Bradshaw circling. She should've used her fingers, anything to silence her body's humming. It wasn't as if she'd see him again, so this attraction had to ease off.

She ran a bath, filling it with the scented oils she'd imported from India. Jasmine and magnolia merged with the tendrils of steam. Drawing in a deep breath, she unbuttoned her blouse, sliding it off her shoulders. She shivered when the heated air touched her skin, but she didn't stop, tugging the shirt out of her skirt's waistband and tossing it onto the wooden stool. Shimmying out of her skirt, she dropped it onto her blouse.

Unzipping her wire-and-lace, nude-toned chemise, she massaged her breasts, moaning as the throbbing sensitivity shot darts of need to her pulsing core.

"Damn you, Tom Bradshaw." She sank into the water, allowing it to ease her muscles, and hopefully, her need.

She dozed and topped up the hot water with a twist of the tap with her toes. Her phone dinged, and she reached for it. Who would send her a text at this time of night?

A gasp tore from her at the name on her screen. She wiped water droplets and damp tendrils off her face as if they hindered her ability to see.

This is Tom.

I'd like to see you tomorrow.

Wiping her hands on her towel, she typed with her thumbs. Her heart beat loud enough to drown out Mrs. Lorenzo's reality shows. *How did you get my number?*

The three dots flickered, as if they crossed the vast cosmos, taking their sweet time to show his reply. *When I want something, nothing stands in my way.*

Her hand trembled, and she fumbled with her phone, almost dropping it into the bath. *I'm busy tomorrow.*

That wasn't a lie. On Saturdays, she worked until noon, lunched with her twin sister, Liz, followed by an afternoon at the community center teaching kids to read. Sunday was the Harvest Fair, and she'd volunteered to manage the kissing booth, like she did every year.

His response was quick. *No, you're not.*

A photo loaded of her book lying on his crumpled sheets, his bare leg peeking in from the bottom of the image. Black hair dusted a muscled thigh, the sight of which drew a gasp from her. Holy Tolkien. She pressed the tip of her tongue to her lip and turned her phone to admire him from all angles.

I want to discuss this book...and the author.

"Holy f...physics." She tossed her phone onto her towel and leaped up, sloshing water everywhere. Soap bubbles sloughed off her, but she didn't care. She stepped onto the mat to trample it, a silent scream contorting her mouth. He couldn't know who Gemma James was. It wasn't public knowledge.

Neither was her phone number.

She squealed, her breathing ragged. She had to answer him. If she didn't, he'd know he'd struck a nerve. *I'd love to discuss Gemma James, Mr. Bradshaw. She is one of our most popular authors. There's even a rumor she's from Gainsford.*

Balancing it on the basin while she dried herself, she gave her phone a smug smile before pulling on a nightgown. She straightened the gathered collar, settled the cinched in waist, and fluffed the frilly skirt that ended mid-thigh. In pastel pink, it was a pointless garment due to its sheer fabric. She adored how it made her feel feminine, delicate, and sexy.

Slipping into dainty, befeathered heels, she brushed her teeth, then rubbed her hair dry, staring at her phone, dreading yet hoping he'd reply. Her heart chose a steady rhythm, then would leap and dance, fluttering butterflies in her chest.

The three dots cycled with no response.

Climbing into bed, she lay there, fingers gripping the quilt, and waited.

Do you think she's single?

She laughed, wondering why that had taken so long for him to type. *Gemma could be a man or someone Maude knows.*

LOL. I doubt it. The way she writes arouses me.

She gasped, squirming into her mattress, tempted to ease the ache between her thighs, but strangely reluctant to do so. *I don't think she's your type, Mr. Bradshaw.*

Call me Tom. Dinner at six.

She harrumphed. The audacity of the man. *I didn't agree to dine with you.*

Good night, Amelia.

She slammed her phone onto her nightstand, mumbling and cursing under her breath as she tossed and turned. Part of her wanted to stand him up, the arrogant donkey's backside. The other part wondered what she should wear.

Chapter Four

Fuck, Tom never overslept, yet here he was speeding north, hoping to reach Gainsford before lunchtime. He'd finished Forbidden Nights in the small hours of the morning. It had taken him over an hour to decide to text her. His lead investigator had messaged him with what details he could find on Amelia Perkins at such short notice.

Tom had skimmed most of it, searching for her number. She was single, had never married, and hadn't left the boundaries of Gainsford. Looking at her, he'd have said she was a cosmopolitan woman, Burlesque in her body language, and too classy for small-town life. A detailed report on her would follow next week.

Did he feel guilty having her investigated? No. Like he'd texted her last night, when he wanted some*one*, he went after her. Not that he'd been this gung-ho for a woman in years. Had he jerked off to James's novel? Yes. Shortly after it, he'd taken the photo.

He chuckled, pulling into the first available parking spot outside Mindy's Diner. Gainsford had two eating establishments: the diner and The Rose Garden. He had her schedule on his phone when he'd accused her of lying about her availability. She *was* free for dinner.

Grabbing the book, he climbed out of his car, hiding his smirk when a few women giggled at the sight of him. He was attractive; he worked hard at it. Today, he'd gone for casual, not trying to impress Amelia. It was his strategy to intensify this attraction for as long as she wanted to deny its existence.

A wicked smile curled his lips. She wouldn't last long. Two days max.

The bell above the door tinkled when he entered the diner, and a gray-haired woman rushed to greet him. He smiled, ignoring those gaping at the stranger among them. She put him in a booth at the back of the diner, which suited him fine. He could watch for Amelia, then set his plan in motion.

"Coffee, please, and if you have bacon, eggs, pancakes?" He tried to hide his wince. Breakfast for him was nothing more than a bowl of muesli with organic yogurt. The waitress nodded, the pencil tucked behind her ear bobbing. She paused when he placed the book on the table.

"Rumor has it the author's from Gainsford." He kept his tone casual, almost charming.

She laughed. "My money's on Celeste. She has the experience for those types of stories." The woman pointed to a brunette at the front of the diner, all sleek curves and luscious hair.

Having to assess people as credible witnesses or for jury duty, he studied her body language and subconscious responses. Flipping the book, he narrowed on the word 'persistent.' He doubted Celeste could spell it, let alone pronounce it.

After sipping his coffee, he shook his head. "No, not her."

"As you say, Mister."

Husky laughter penetrated his thoughts, and he raised his gaze to the door. Amelia...dressed in a white vest, leggings, ballet slippers, and a crochet needle pinning her bun on top of her head? On her hip bounced a miniature version of her: pale skin, pink cheeks, and red curls. She hurried toward him, sinking into the seat two booths from his.

"The usual, Lizzy?" The waitress picked up the toddler to cuddle.

Twins? Air rushed out of his lungs, and he slumped into the seat. For a moment there, he'd thought his lead investigator had the wrong information. She looked like Amelia, except for the lack of lipstick, coiffed hair, and simmering sensuality.

"Yes, please, Mindy. Kimmy's a bit of a handful this morning." Lizzy flicked tendrils of auburn hair out of her face.

"Amy's on her way?" Mindy lowered Kimmy onto the seat. "Should I order for her?"

Lizzy nodded. "She's outside on a call."

Electricity zinged through him, and he shifted his ass, trying to ease the growing ache in his groin. Not that he removed his gaze from the sidewalk or bothered to look at Mindy when she brought him coffee.

When the door opened and the bell tinkled, the tension in the room thickened until he couldn't breathe. In tight tailored pants, ending mid-calf, a sleeveless, V-necked, black-and-white polka-dot top, and dangerous peep-toe platforms, Amelia oozed sex appeal. She'd left her hair down like yesterday, curling to the side, and wore the same ruby lipstick. He shuffled across the seat to the shadowed corner. If he offered her his back, he wouldn't see her, wouldn't watch the fabric shift across her hips, or the enticing jostle of her breasts as she sashayed.

"Aunty Amy." The little girl scampered across the checkered floor of the diner.

Amelia slid her glasses onto her head and dipped to scoop the girl into her arms. Tiny hands touched where he longed to, but more breathtaking was Amelia's smile.

"Hey, sweetheart, how's my favorite girl?"

That husky voice stilled his heart, and right then, he knew, he was in trouble. He should leave now, should walk away from something that could change his life. Not that he could foresee if it was a positive or negative impact. Regardless, his legs wouldn't move, deciding the matter for him.

Onto his table, Mindy slid a plate of bacon and eggs, then a side plate stacked high with syrup-drenched pancakes. He smiled at her. Drawing in a deep breath, he squared his shoulders. He was a grown man. How much trouble could one plump librarian be? Visions of her sprawled beneath him had him clenching his cutlery until the cold stainless steel dug into his palms.

When her laughter filling the diner as Kimmy kissed her cheeks, he raised his gaze. He focused his hearing, trying to eavesdrop on their conversation.

"So, you're free this afternoon? That would make anyone else happy." Lizzy dunked a fry into ketchup and offered it to Kimmy.

"I suppose it only sets my program back a week." Amelia sighed as she stroked a curl off Kimmy's cheek. "Still, I'd have liked to have been part of the discussion."

"The fair's tomorrow, and you know they need hands. These kids receive a free meal and wages for the day." Lizzy laughed, reaching across to pat Amelia's hand. "I love your passion for literacy, sis, but give them a break."

"You're right, Liz, as always." Amelia peppered kisses across Kimmy's neck, drawing contagious giggles from the little girl. "Want to swap places like we used to?"

"Oh, now that's tempting." Lizzy bit into a fry. "Dave made me swear never to do that. He claims you intimidate him."

"I do not. It's just that…" She rose to bounce Kimmy on her hip, juggling her breasts in the process. Tom refused to blink. "I have to do the kissing booth every d…Dewey year."

Liz smirked. "You can't back out for sh…sure."

He grinned. Neither sisters liked to swear. There had to be a story behind that.

"I *have* a backbone." Amelia huffed, slid onto the seat, and shifted the little girl beside her.

"How many book clubs do you chair?" Liz held a cup of milk for Kimmy.

Amelia shook her head, cascading her thick auburn curls. "As the head librarian—"

Liz held up her palm. "And who dated Dirty Niles?"

Pressing her hand over her chest, Amelia smiled. "It was just one night, and he looked so pathetic, I couldn't—"

"As I said, you can't back out on anything, sis."

"You're right." She handed Kimmy to Liz, then dug her phone out of her back pocket. "Hello, Mrs. Arnold. Yes, about tomorrow… No, I can't… Oh, I see. How bad is it? For a week? No, no, tomorrow's fine. Of course, I'm looking forward to it too. Goodbye."

Lizzy arched both brows as if to say, 'I told you so.'

"My substitute fell into an open manhole and is in the hospital. She fractured both legs." Amelia's shoulders shook, and she chuckled. "I'm sorry, it's not funny." Then she burst into a husky laugh.

Lizzy joined her until tears streamed down her cheeks. "Like I said—"

"Yes, Mom." Amelia held up her palms. "Next year, I'll make sure I'm out of town for all the fairs."

"There we go, problem solved." Liz grinned. "Still a coward, though."

Amelia threw a fry at her sister.

He smothered a laugh with a cough and pulled out his phone to text her, wanting to see her reactions. *Looking forward to tonight.*

Amelia froze, raising her hand to her flushed cheek as she read his text.

Her fingers trembled as she typed, *I have plans.*

If I have your number, I have your address. Do you want me in your home and near your bed, Amelia?

She gasped and cupped the phone to her chest.

"What's wrong?" Liz frowned.

Amelia flicked a dismissive hand. "Nothing, just dealing with some hotshot..." *Fine, I'll meet you at the Rose Garden. Dinner, nothing more.*

He smothered the bark of laughter this victory summoned in him. *Nothing more until you ask nicely.*

She squeaked and tossed her phone onto the seat.

He chuckled, enjoying tormenting her.

"So, what did Doc. Brown say?" Amelia twirled her straw in her pink milkshake then sucked on it. A long pull of need mimicked her actions, from his belly to his cock. He shuddered, dropping his focus to his half-eaten breakfast. He couldn't recall the taste of bacon, yet not a piece remained.

Liz shrugged, popping another fry into her mouth. "That I'm five weeks pregnant."

"What?" Amelia gaped, the pink of her mouth enticing his gaze to linger again. She leaped out to hug her sister. A bright smile sparked joy across her face, and tears shimmered on her eyelashes.

"Dave's hoping for a boy." Liz's grin didn't rouse the same reaction within Tom.

Amelia slouched, then sighed before straightening her posture. "No fair. You have the best man in town. I can't even find someone to f...*physics* with."

"At some point, your lover would stumble upon your closet, sis. The poor man." Liz giggled, mimicking shock and horror with her hand across her mouth.

Pink crawled across Amelia's cheeks. "Yes, well, everyone collects something." She fidgeted with the napkin then dabbed her mouth with it.

"Shoes, books, movies, hell, even stamps would be preferable." Liz fanned herself as if she was hot and bothered.

Now he was curious. Would Amelia have something sexual in that closet? The heads of her past lovers? He chuckled at his macabre thoughts. If all things went according to plan, he'd find out soon enough. Until then, he'd continue to toy with her.

He tossed money onto the table and rose, pausing beside their booth. Both women raised startled gazes to him, but he focused on Amelia. Her cheeks flushed again, the color spreading to her cleavage, and those delicious lips parted on an 'oh.' She ran her walnut-brown gaze over his jeans, the noticeable bulge he didn't try to hide, and his navy T-shirt.

He didn't care that the diner's customers watched him, that Liz gaped, glancing between him and Amelia.

Placing a splayed hand on the table, and one behind her, close enough to bury his fingers in her hair, he dipped to brush his lips across her ear. Fuck, she smelled so good. When he sucked in a sharp breath, his nostrils flared. He succumbed and nipped her earlobe. Her moan hardened his cock until it pulsed to his heartbeat.

"Tonight, Amelia. Wear something sexy...," he lingered his gaze for longer than was necessary on her heaving breasts, "...or wear nothing at all."

He dropped the book onto her lap, and she yelped, her body trembling. Chuckling at the progress he made, he strolled out, not bothering to confirm she and all Mindy's customers gawked. Yes, two days max, and he'd have sultry, seductive, alluring, and irresistible Amelia Perkins beneath him.

Chapter Five

"WHO THE F...FRIDGE WAS that?" Liz twisted in the booth to watch Tom stroll out.

Amy couldn't speak, doubted she could rasp a word. Holy Hemingway, she wasn't equipped to handle him, this...whatever this was that had her heart thumping and her breathing erratic.

Liz tapped Amy's cheek. "Who, Amy? Speak."

"Maude's grandson." Amy sucked on her strawberry milkshake as if it was her lifeline to sanity.

"Maude's...? Did you see the way he looked at you?" Liz gaped. "I could smell him from here, and I mean, in a good way, like sex-on-a-stick, lick-his-lollipop way."

"Liz," Amy gasped, cupping her palms over Kimmy's ears. When her dear sister bit into her burger, Amy released Kimmy with a kiss to her temple. "He doesn't like Maude's choice of reading material and would like to discuss it tonight."

Using the book to fan herself, she imagined the cover still held the warmth of his hand. She shivered, wishing she'd worn something a little roomier. Every shift of her backside rubbed her sweetheart blouse across her sensitive nipples.

"He won't take no for an answer." She huffed. "Did you see him? He reeks of one-night-stands. Been there, have the closet for it."

"I saw him all right, so did all of Gainsford. You might as well test him out because everyone thinks you've done him already." Liz threw down a few banknotes and started gathering hers and Kimmy's things. "I want every sensual, breath-snatching detail, y'hear?"

"It's not happening, Liz. You know why." Amy scooped Kimmy into her arms for a quick cuddle before handing her niece to her mother.

"Make it happen. Some of us live vicariously through you." With Kimmy on her hip, Liz paused. "I'll call on Monday."

Sighing, Amy pushed her uneaten burger to the side and opened Forbidden Nights. She thumbed through the pages, remembering the long hours of writing and editing. Black pen snagged her attention, and she gasped. Who would dare deface a library book?

This...with you, your alabaster skin, and dark sultry eyes.

F! Do this to me, the heat of your mouth, the soft warmth of your tongue.

She couldn't breathe, imagining Tom naked in bed, writing these words, knowing she'd find them. As seduction techniques went, he was a master. Fury took a backseat since she could replace the book from her personal stock.

She was drowning here, lost in an ocean of sensation. There was no lifeline, other than to sink to the bottom and let the turbulent waves thrash above her. Drawing in a slow breath, she willed her heartbeat to calm. She'd meet him for dinner then goodbye. He could fluster her, he could stalk her, he could torment her with his texts, his proximity, and his charming smile, but she was made of sturdier stuff. He'd grow bored and move on, like all players did. She just had to hold out until then.

A broken heart, splintered dreams, and having to watch her sister with Dave meant she'd confined herself to a miserable life. That she intimidated Dave had her reeling. She wanted to wail and laugh, but in the end, she'd just sob into her pillow.

When he'd moved here, she'd loved him at first sight and hurried to welcome him to Gainsford. Faulkner save her, she'd even invited him to dinner with her sister, not knowing how they'd connect. Before her horrified gaze, Liz blossomed, Dave gushed, and they'd shattered Amy's naïve hopes.

To hide how hurt she was, she became a tough-as-nails bitch to him, and now, couldn't change his perception of her. Nor could she stop her snide comments stemming from bitterness. If she was honest with herself, they wouldn't have suited each other. Dave was too mild for her personality, but still, as the only decent-looking man in town...

At least, Lizzy had him. There was a small consolation in that.

Mindy cleared the table, tossing knowing smiles at her. "Who was that?"

As the head of the gossip circle, Mindy knew everyone's business. There was no lying to the woman or attempts to evade her.

"Maude's grandson." Amy pasted on a smile, pretending a nonchalance she was far from feeling.

"That great brute came from Maude's tiny daughter-in-law?"

Amy shrugged. What could she say to that? He was tall and built like a lumberjack.

"What did he want with you?" Mindy fanned herself with a dirty napkin. "I damn near swallowed my gum when he kissed you."

Gasping, Amy clutched the book to her chest. Sure, she yearned for a kiss, but she couldn't have the townsfolk believing he had. "He didn't kiss me just whispered to me. He's super pis...passionate about Maude's choice of books and wants me to censor her."

"Right, like any of us can stand up to Maude Bradshaw." Mindy laughed. "You come running here if he gives you any trouble. My Ol' Hank will sort him out."

Amy closed her eyes, fighting for calm. "He's not bullying me."

"That's not what I saw." Mindy harrumphed.

"He's persuasive and single-minded as all city folk are." Amy forced a chuckle when all she wanted to do was sink into her bed with a pillow over her head. "He's taking me to dinner tonight to state his case, which I'm sure is detailed. I'm not scared of him, but thank you for the sweet offer."

"That boy wants you, Amelia Perkins. Mark my words."

Amy blinked, bombarded with images of Tom seducing her. Her breathing faltered, but under Mindy's vigilant gaze, she had to pretend she was the purest spinster in a hundred-mile radius.

"I...don't know, Mindy. If he does, what do I do?" She gaped like a fish out of water. Was she overdoing it? Hell, yes. The people of Gainsford thought her a virgin. It had taken her years to end their pitying glances after Dave broke her heart, and no sexy stallion of a banker would jeopardize it.

Mindy patted her hand. "I can ask Niles to escort you to and from The Rose Garden?"

Amy smothered a giggle. Pitting Niles against Tom would be like an earthworm battling a cobra. "Oh, that's so kind of you, but it might put Mr. Bradshaw on the defensive. I need him to leave me alone on his own."

"Mm, you may be right. He looked awfully strong and might hurt my overzealous son." Mindy took the money on the table and pocketed it. "You have my thanks for agreeing to a date with Niles. He said you were such a bitch that he's over you."

"It was a brilliant plan, Mindy, and if I can't handle this banker, then I'll come to you." Amy slid out of the booth and left the diner. On the bus home, she discarded strategies and their possible outfits.

By the time she walked through her front door, she had somewhat of a plan in mind. She would dress to kill, flirt, and laugh with long, lingering glances. Tit for tat, so to speak. By the end of the evening, she hoped to have him harder than the Rock of Gibraltar. Then she'd walk away. Besides, she had a stunning red dress she hadn't worn in a while.

Tom Bradshaw was a challenge and one she shouldn't shy away from. She wanted to see how far she could push him until he revealed his true agenda. He'd gone from censoring 'filth' to tormenting her. Sexual innuendo didn't help with his original goal, so switching tactics didn't make sense.

As long as he didn't fluster her like he had at the diner, then she'd be fine.

Chapter Six

Tom smiled at the caller on his phone, and warmth spread across his chest. "Hi, Gram."

"Don't 'hi' me, my boy. What's this I hear you're harassing Amelia?" The cultured voice of his gram shrieked across the connection.

He laughed, pulling the phone away from his ear. "Harassing? Is that what she calls it?" He hadn't expected her to run to his only surviving relative, but it was a battle strategy he admired.

She huffed. "Sweet Amy? No, Mindy, dumbass. This is a small town, and you damn near kissed the girl."

Oh, so not Amelia. He couldn't decide if he was disappointed or if her keeping it between them meant he had reason to hope. "We were debating, Gram, whether she ought to be letting you read such filth."

He grimaced, casting a glance at the bookshop bag on his passenger seat. It was far from filth, but it would take a frozen day in hell before he admitted he was wrong.

"She's a stunner, isn't she, Tom?" The softness of Gram's voice fired his instincts.

He slumped, pressing his temple to the steering wheel. Was this all a ruse? Gram trying to hook him up with a woman she thought was perfect for him?

Visions of Amelia Perkins not far from his thoughts rose to torment him. His heart rate spiked, and he nodded. "She is." He cleared his throat, something hard squeezing his chest. "Tell me you're not matchmaking, Gram, please?"

"I'm not. I moved here to be with my friends, Tom, and this town has welcomed me with open arms. I can't afford to have you swinging your pecker around and causing havoc."

He mouthed 'swinging your pecker' then yelped when someone tapped on his car window. An elderly woman arched her brows in a look he'd been the recipient of for almost three decades. Sighing, he powered the window down, tilting his head as if to offer her his ear for boxing.

She hung up the call with a trembling forefinger. "Quit being such a jackass. I lived through the seventies. You don't think I know what an orgasm is? How the hell do you think I fell pregnant with your father? Immaculate Conception wasn't popular in my day."

"Gram, I wasn't harassing her, honest. She needs tighter control over who reads what. For all you know, a pre-teen has read these books." He gestured for her to step aside and climbed out of the car. Then with a naughty smile, he lifted her off her feet for a crushing hug, like he hadn't done this just yesterday.

She pummeled his shoulders then returned the hug. "Put me down, you scamp."

He did, still grinning at her when he locked the car and trailed after her.

"You bullied her for a date tonight, didn't you?" She lowered herself onto a nearby bench, pulling her pastel purple cardigan around her frail body.

"Of course." He sprawled beside her, throwing an arm around her shoulders to share his warmth. A slight breeze ruffled the daisies, and he didn't want her catching a cold.

"I adore you, always have, but Amelia's too good for you, my boy." Gram cackled, laughter scrunching her hazel eyes. "She'll chew you up and spit you out."

His cock twitched, and he shifted, twisting his pelvis to hide the growing bulge from a too-observant grandmother. He'd love for Amelia to chew on any part of him, and therein lay the excitement. He hadn't chased after a woman in years. They tended to throw themselves at his feet, like bras at a rock concert.

"Come to dinner. You can state your case..."

Gram rested her signature glare on him again. "My choice of reading material is none of your business. It's called freedom, Tom, something a lawyer should know about."

"It's called concern. I'm entitled to my opinion, Gram."

"And I'm entitled not to listen to it." She huffed, her gnarled fingers tightening on her skirt, crumpling the fabric. "How long are you staying in town?"

"A few days." A slow smile crawled across his face, reflecting off Gram's reading glasses. He expected tonight to be worth suffering the lust bombarding him at unexpected moments...like now.

Gram snorted. "I still have this fandangled phone you bought me. Text me. I want progress reports."

He groaned, sitting up straight. "You *did* set me up."

She pressed her palm to her chest. "I did not, but entertainment is television or gossip in Gainsford. The girls and I could do with a giggle when you fail."

"You have no confidence in me." He scowled. His own grandmother thought he couldn't get the girl.

"Listen, I'm going to hear about your endeavors, and I'd rather know the truth than whatever Mindy can concoct." Gram giggled, rubbing her hands together with glee. The humor crinkling her hazel eyes melted his resolve.

He sighed. "Fair enough."

Gripping his forearm, she pulled herself onto her wobbling feet. "Now, off you go. I need a nap, and you have a stash of filth to read." She snorted. "Didn't think I'd see those?" She shook her head. "Dumbass."

Heat warmed his cheeks, and he couldn't remember when last he'd blushed.

She kissed his temple and toddled off.

"Gram, wait." He bolted off the bench, closing the distance between them. "Rumor has it that Gemma James lives in Gainsford. Any ideas who the author might be?"

She gaped then giggled. "What a conundrum. I'll ask around. The girls and I will figure it out, my boy." She patted his arm and walked toward the waiting nurse.

Fuck, now he had to report in. What if there wasn't progress? No, he couldn't think like that. He'd targeted models, socialites, married women, so one lonely, most-likely virginal librarian shouldn't be a problem.

Yet, he couldn't help but feel Amelia wasn't buying what he was selling. Sure, she reacted to him as a man, but he didn't think she'd succumb so easily to his charms. He hoped not. He was enjoying the chase too much to want it to end sooner than two days.

Climbing into the car, he pulled the book bag onto his lap, sorting through its contents. He'd head to his room, curl into bed, and start book two of Masculine Manipulation. Even the name of the series was tongue-in-cheek. Closer to six, he'd shower and put on his best suit. He'd thought of wearing his dark-blue jacket with jeans, but he wanted to impress her. So he'd wear a dark-blue suit and a white shirt, unbuttoned and gaping for her delectation.

He chuckled, started his engine, and reversed.

Time to set his plans in motion.

Chapter Seven

Amy twisted to admire her reflection in the mirror. She'd swept her hair into an updo, pinning thick curls on top. The scarlet satin dress hugged her figure, cinching in at her waist and accentuating every curve to below her knees in a semi-mermaid style. The sweetheart neckline thrust her breasts up with large swaths of pale skin shimmering in the lamplight.

Eyeliner, mascara, and scarlet lipstick were her war paint. A faux-fur shawl, elbow-length satin gloves, and vintage clutch—all in black—finished the ensemble along with her black platform pumps, adding a lovely shape to her calves. She had book lifting to thank for their muscle mass, so at least her fat didn't wobble when she walked.

At her front door, she listened for Mrs. Lorenzo, not wanting to have a chat this evening. Amy believed that punctuality was a sign of respect. Any deviance from this irritated her and ruined her day. With a reality show blaring next door, she hurried out of her home to the single garage.

Whenever she looked at her prizanged possession, a 1957 Chevrolet Bel Air convertible, her heart fluttered, and she'd run a gloved finger along its gleaming teal fender. Its restoration had cost a small fortune. She climbed into the driver's seat, adjusting her backside on the white leather. That afternoon, she'd taken the time to pull up the canopy so she wouldn't have to protect her hair.

As she wallowed in admiration for her car and how stunning she looked, she tried not to focus on the evening ahead in Tom's company. Her skin prickled, as if it couldn't decide to shiver or perspire. Her heart rate skittered, leaped, danced, leaving her a little breathless. When she gripped the steering wheel, her fingers trembled.

Magnolia wafted across the breeze, and she sighed. She'd foregone perfume this evening because she'd had a long soak in her flower-scented bath, using the time to calm her nerves.

By now, everyone knew where she was heading and with whom she'd dine. It wouldn't surprise her if one of her neighbors phoned the owners, the Petersons, to let them know she was on her way.

"Get a grip, Amelia Perkins." She huffed and reversed the car, pulling into the empty street. "What can he do? Charm you to death?"

With his square jaw, those perfect lips, and brooding hazel eyes? Mm, she ought to enjoy the delicious eye candy he was and think no further than that. Of course, a small town meant short distances, and she pulled into the parking at The Rose Garden a few minutes before six, halfway through a Rammstein. She'd needed their rough vocals to bolster her courage.

There was still time to turn around, to make up an excuse, but she wasn't a coward. She climbed out of the car, gathered her shawl around her, and strolled into the restaurant.

"Good evening, Amy." Barbara Peterson smiled, her pinned-up gray hair sharpening her cheekbones. She had aged well, which had more to do with her sense of humor. "I hear you're battling quite the devil."

Amy chuckled. "He's far from that. Just a concerned grandson." She scanned the restaurant's patrons, searching for her... Holy Whitman, she's almost thought of him as her date.

"He's waiting at the bar." With a wide sweep of her arm, Barbara stepped aside.

Offering a smile of thanks, Amy strode into the dimly lit enclosed section for those interested in company and a drink rather than dinner. It took her a moment to locate Tom.

Her breath hitched. She trailed her gaze over his tall masculine body in a tapered navy-blue suit. He'd worn brown shoes with a matching belt. His shirt was a little too tight, molding a chest no banker should have—the white contrasted with his olive skin tone.

His shoulders looked impossibly wide, drawing her gaze to his dark hair curled over the jacket's collar. Sighing, she settled on his face, and her heartbeat froze for a few seconds before skittering to catch up. He'd watched her drool over him.

He *was* a handsome man and had to be used to women ogling him like he was chocolate. Despite the burn on her cheeks, she squared her shoulders, maintained eye contact, and weaved through the crowd toward him.

Parts of her tingled, heat sprinkling along her skin as if his gaze lingered. She blamed her nerves mixing with the air-conditioning.

He cupped her elbow and crowded her between his body and the bar counter as if to shield her. Then he ruined the feeling of protection by leaning in to brush his lips across her ear. Shards of iced fire slithered down her spine and puckered her nipples.

"Fuck, you look stunning." Pausing, he groaned, dipping his chin into the curve of her neck to draw in a long inhale. "Smell incredible too."

He feathered his fingers up her arm, stopping when he encountered her skin, as if he didn't like the gloves. She fought the urge to tug them off and shove them into her clutch. No, she'd do that before dinner, but not now, not needing his touch to inflame her blood.

"Something to drink, or are you hungry?" He pressed in on her, his intoxicating cologne spinning her thoughts. She wanted to rest her temple on his lapel and burrow into his embrace.

Tolkien have mercy. She jerked then stepped back, having almost succumbed. "A sherry, please."

He placed the order, nursing a glass of something golden on ice. She frowned, not liking a man to drink, but then again, she couldn't judge. She didn't know how long he'd been there and how many glasses he'd had.

A small sip of sherry was all she allowed herself, but the way her nerves coiled in her stomach tempted her to throw back the fiery liquid. She tightened her fingers around the delicate glass. "Did I keep you waiting?"

"Not at all. I arrived a few minutes ago and chose to wait here." He grinned, his teeth bright against his swarthy cheeks. "Shall we?" He left his unfinished drink, and she hurried to do the same.

"Put it on my tab, Jamie." She smiled at the young bartender.

"Will do, Ms. Perkins." He gave her a wicked grin and flicked his towel onto his shoulder.

Tom tightened his fingers on her elbow, and he tugged her a little too forcefully beside him. "You're with me tonight, Amelia."

"Huh?" She frowned, not understanding his implications. A pulse ticked at the base of his jaw as he ushered her to their table.

He pulled out a chair for her, making sure she had her back to the bar, then tossed out a glare. Was he jealous? Of Jamie? She pinched her lips, trying to smother a laugh.

"What do you find amusing?" He lowered his bulk into his chair, draping the napkin across his lap.

"That was a splendid display of jealousy, Mr. Bradshaw." She laughed, uncaring whether she offended him.

"I wasn't..." He paused, then sighed. "Yes, I was."

"He's been with Mike for two years now. Caused quite a scandal at the time."

Tom gave her a curt nod. "Shall we discuss the purpose of this dinner?"

She stilled, his formal tone ending her good humor. Right, this wasn't a date. "The answer is no." She gathered her shawl around her, regretting wasting the afternoon preparing her mind and body. Anticipation had driven her, perhaps boredom along with the enticement of a sensual man she wouldn't have minded sampling...just once.

"No to discussing the purpose?"

"No to censoring Maude's reading material." She rose. "Good night, Mr. Bradshaw."

"Sit, Amelia." His tone brooked no argument, still, she hesitated to obey. "My grand-mother has made her opinion known on that subject." He gestured to the chair.

Amy placed her clutch on the table and slid into the chair with a frown. He could've called and canceled. "Then the purpose of this dinner is...?"

"Do you want the truth or something in the middle?" He waved his fingers and ordered a bottle of water for the table.

"The truth." What was this man up to? If this evening wasn't to discuss the filth in her library, then why waste her time?

He rested his elbows on the table and drew in a long breath. "I find myself in a strange situation."

She said nothing, waiting for him to continue. Her shawl slipped, and she flicked it over the back of the chair. Then she rested her elbow on the table and her chin in her palm. She took the opportunity to admire the exact shape of his nose, those perfect Michelangelo-inspired lips, and his mesmerizing hazel eyes.

His jaw clenched, and his gaze traversed her bare shoulders, lingering on her mouth. She fought the urge to roll her now-tingling lips inward, to hide from his attention.

"I want you." His mile-wide shoulders relaxed a little, as if it had taken all of his strength to speak.

"To do what, Mr. Bradshaw?" She shifted, dropping her arms to her side to hide her fidgeting fingers. Had she not been a spinster, she might have read something into those three little words. Her heart had skipped a beat, but she hurried to remind herself he hadn't meant it sexually.

"Dammit, Amelia, call me Tom." His rasping voice skittered along her skin, and she shivered.

"Very well, *Tom*, what do you want me to do for you?"

He waited while Cathy poured water into their glasses, settled the bottle into a nearby ice bucket, and left. The breadsticks remained untouched.

He leaned across the table, closing the distance between them. "I want *you*."

She arched a brow, trying for nonchalance when she was far from it. Those same cliché butterflies she described in her novels assaulted her stomach, and she gripped the tablecloth, hoping he didn't notice. "It sounds like you mean in an intimate way, Tom." Was that breathless voice hers?

The slow smile that crawled across his lips was nothing short of spectacular. Her core pulsed in immediate response, and she shifted in the chair to ease the ache.

His gaze dropped to her sweetheart neckline before flicking up to meet hers. "Yes, as intimate as possible."

Heat burst across her cheeks, her neck, and down to her breasts. "Why?" Sure, she'd received offers for sexual release from many men, just none so blatant nor as sexy.

"I want to taste your skin, Amelia, your lips."

She gasped, then gave up trying to breathe normally. "I'm not blonde, skinny or…um, as experienced." She lowered her gaze to her quivering breasts.

"Are you trying to explain why I shouldn't have a raging hard-on for you?" He laughed. "This is a courtesy. I'm letting you know my intentions."

Cathy hovered nearby. Fresh heat splashed Amy's cheeks at the thought that she might overhear their conversation. "I'll have the usual, Cathy."

"Make that two." Tom didn't look at the poor waitress but captured Amy's gloved hand.

Time passed as he ran his thumb across her knuckles. He waited and watched, his gaze trailing fire over her shoulders and face.

"Thank you for telling me." She smothered a hysterical giggle, as joy, fear, and nerves bubbled up her throat. What was she supposed to say? She'd love a good fuck? How sweet of him to consider her for the position?

A tug on her hand drew her attention, and he pulled off the glove, one finger at a time before dropping it onto the table. He pressed her fingertips to his soft lips. She twitched, surprised at the tingles shooting along her skin.

"Better," he said, his voice gravel again.

"You're trying to seduce me, Tom." She laughed. "Does this usually work for you?"

He shook his head. "I don't need to put out any effort."

"Oh, poor you." She tugged her hand free when Cathy arrived with the plates of pasta.

"Why do I feel you're not considering my offer?" He frowned, and that brooding intensity was back.

Fool. If she did take him seriously, she'd fall hard, and her heart hadn't healed from the last time. Was fear driving her to run? Hell, yes.

"Why should I?" She gestured to Cathy. "Please pack this to go, and put the meal on my tab." She pulled on the glove then rose. "Thank you for an entertaining evening, Mr. Bradshaw. May I never see you again."

With her shawl across her shoulders along with a mantle of dignity and loneliness, she ignored Tom as she waited for her takeaway. With a smile to Cathy, she headed for her car. She opened the passenger door first, placed the meal, her shawl, gloves, and clutch on top of the seat, then closed the door. When she looped around the hood, Tom waited for her.

"You would swear no woman has ever said no to you." She sighed. "You're a player, a one-night-stand jockey. You're chasing an orgasm, fake or otherwise; what does it matter?"

He bolted forward and pinned her with his hips to her car. His cologne, his body's edges, hard muscle, and heat engulfed her senses, and she moaned. Yet she didn't break eye contact, trying to stay strong against the temptation of him. Would he rock her world? *Yes*. Would she recover from it? *No*.

He cupped her chin, slid his fingers along her jaw until he buried them in her hair, cascading pins as he loosened her updo. Then with a solid nudge, he tilted her face to meet his as he descended his lips to her mouth.

She squirmed, wishing she could break the mesmerizing swirl of his hazel eyes, which appeared bluer tonight.

"I want to fuck you, Amelia Perkins." His breath whispered across her lips, and she shivered. "Please, let me."

Had he kissed her, she might have melted into a pathetic puddle at his feet.

"Fine." She cleared her throat and scraped her nails up his nape to bury her fingers in his hair. Then she thrashed her head, tossed her hair wild, and released a throaty moan. Gasping and panting, she hitched her breath then peppered it with whispers of his name amid pleas for him to not stop.

He stilled, his grip on her jaw tightening, and he shuddered when she continued as if she was in the throes of an exquisite orgasm. Her cries of release reverberated across the parking lot. Rubbing her breasts against his chest was par for the course, even though molten lust liquified in her core. She ached and yearned, but inconsiderate and cowardly wisdom prevailed.

On a drawn-out sigh, she patted his shoulder. "There we go, one fake orgasm. My gift to you." She thrust forward with her hips, encountering something incredibly hard. Surprising him gave her a sliver of space. She took it, opened her car door, and slid in.

"Good night, Mr. Bradshaw, and goodbye." Did she feel vindicated for all women when she drove away from him? *Yes.* Did she mourn a lost evening of wild, once-in-a-life-time, abandoned passion? *Also, yes.*

She watched him in the rearview mirror, standing there in the middle of the parking lot. He seemed lost, and pity curled around the wall of ice around her heart. No, she wouldn't feel sorry for him. She was nothing but a warm body.

Still, having an earthshattering orgasm would've been nice.

She sighed. Tonight, she'd open her infamous closet.

~*~

What the fuck just happened? Tom rubbed a trembling hand over his face, curse words on the tip of his tongue that he'd swallowed the moment she'd sashayed out of the restaurant.

Fuck, that red against her skin, those delicious curves, and her breasts close to slipping free. When he'd touched her waist, it wasn't a corset that cinched it in. Her figure was a true hourglass, and as he reviewed his responses, he adored her peaks and valleys.

He'd messed this up, unable to use his suave words on her. She'd blindsided him with her air of untouchability when that was exactly what he wanted to do—touch her all over. He hadn't lied when he said he wanted to taste her.

Her perfume was on her skin, the scent of which clung to his lips from when he'd kissed her fingertips. Hell, she'd quivered, her reactions an open book. One-night-stand jockey? He was, but it wasn't often that he mourned the loss of such a night and the chance at such a woman.

And her fake orgasm. Holy fuck. She'd touched his neck, scraped her nails across his scalp, and moaned as if he'd sucked on her nipple, or dipped his fingers between her thighs. His muscles had frozen, and his throat squeezed shut, not that he could form a thought. He throbbed, he ached, his cock twitched as if to say he'd promised relief, but where the hell was it?

He watched until her taillights disappeared then stomped inside. First, he settled the tab, trying to take back some of the control he'd lost the moment she'd walked into the bar. Minutes later, sitting in his car, he stared at the food container on his seat, the pasta cold and congealed. Now what?

Pulling his phone out of his inside jacket pocket, he dialed Gram.

"It's bad." He pinched the bridge of his nose, trying to think of a way to sway Amelia, to convince her to spread those delicious thighs. His nipples puckered, and he growled, activating the speaker to remove his jacket.

"I know. Rumor has it you ogled her like a leprechaun who found the jackpot."

"Pretty much." He thumped his temple on the steering wheel. "I was overconfident, I admit it."

He picked up his phone, deactivated the speaker functionality, and pressed it to his ear.

"What happened to the charming boy who had all the neighborhood's whores chasing after him?" Gram sighed. "What did you do or say to drive sweet Amelia to leave your ass?"

"I told her I wanted her."

"Ah, Tom, where's the magic in that? If you were here, I'd box your ears." Gram grumbled something as if her hand was over the phone. She put him on mute, then screamed in his ear after figuring out how to unmute. "I got you on speaker."

Fucking great.

"Tomorrow's the fair," another woman said. "Try the kissing booth."

"Elise, she doesn't do the kissing." Gram's tone was as dry as dust. "She manages it, birdbrain."

"With the right monetary incentive, our dear Tom could find his lips on hers for a juicy smacker." Elise made a smooching sound as if she were a ten-year-old boy.

"I take that back, Elise. That's brilliant." The black screen shimmered, and Gram's nose filled the camera. "It's a dollar a kiss or some such nonsense. Offer more to kiss Amelia."

"How much more?" He pasted on a smile in case Gram realized she'd activated the video call. What he wanted was to drown his sorrows in something lethal, like scotch.

"How much is it worth to you?" Gram's hairy chin made its debut appearance. "Or leave and never bother again. You either want her or you don't."

"I remember, Gram. A Bradshaw does nothing half-cocked." He winced. If she only knew how full-cocked he was. Full, hard, aching, drooling...any kind of description he could think of to describe how aroused he was.

He'd imagined a different outcome to this evening, not a cold dinner and a colder shower. "I'm heading to my room, Gram and ladies. I'll call you after the fair."

"Okay," Gram said, her wide smile flashing her dentures. "It starts at nine and ends at sunset. Time it well."

He nodded. "Love you."

Tossing the phone onto the seat, he turned the key in the ignition.

"Good night, Mr. Bradshaw, and goodbye." Amelia's last words haunted him. She had no idea how she'd challenged him by driving away as if she hadn't felt the connection between them. He'd read her reactions correctly, reciprocated them, as well.

He rolled his tense shoulders, gripped the steering wheel, and released a controlled breath. She'd find out tomorrow that he wasn't letting her go.

Chapter Eight

TOM WAS A FOOL. Not only had he read into the small hours of the morning, but he'd also gone for a jog past her house, twice. The first time, he'd needed to know where the shadows were to spare her from the gossip. Gram had been right to remind him that they lived in a small town, and everything he did impacted her.

On the last jog home, he'd wondered why Amelia's lights were on. Was she entertaining someone? A man he didn't know about? Her conversation with Liz confirmed she was single, but people lied to their families all the time. It bothered him so much that he slipped around to her backyard.

Did he circle her home? Without a doubt.

Did he watch her at her desk, typing away, sipping sherry in a delicate nightgown that left nothing to the imagination? To his distress, yes.

Sweat drenched his vest, so there was no demanding entry and seducing Amelia. Instead, he ogled her through the glass panes of her enclosed patio like a stalker. She must have sensed him since he hadn't made a noise.

Her head shot up, and she gaped. Fuck, without painting her lips ruby or pink, she was still gorgeous. She chewed on her bottom lip as if she knew what he was thinking. Then, flipping her laptop closed, she rose, veered around her antique desk, and faced him, an inch away from the glass.

He lowered his gaze, fascinated by the hint of her dark nipples through the pink diaphanous fabric. Her skin glowed, and her robe accentuated rather than hid her from his focus. He imagined gathering the hem, crushing the fabric as he glided his hand over her thigh, hip, into the dent of her waist to cup a breast.

He pressed his palm to the window, needing to touch her and the chilliness of the glass to ground him.

A delicate furrow formed on her brow. Shaking her head, tossing her unbound curls in the process, she side-stepped and unlocked the sliding door.

"Tom, what are you doing here?"

He grinned. Flames of lust shot through him, and he fought the urge to gather her close to him. She'd more than sealed her fate with her husky voice rolling his name off her tongue.

"I couldn't sleep. I wanted to apologize." He didn't ask to enter her home. She had to make the choice, and if she did, it opened her to so much more.

She folded her arms across her chest, thrusting her breasts up. Her nipples pebbled, and for the first time, he realized how cold it was outside. Heat from her fire flushed his cheeks, but he didn't budge.

"For what are you sorry, Mr. Bradshaw?"

He scowled. "Tom, please, Amelia."

Sighing, she dropped her arms and swished the skirts of her nightgown. Fuck, she was absolutely naked beneath it. The fabric pressed against dark red curls at the junction of her thighs before falling into place.

"Tom, this is insane. Leave before someone sees you. I work hard on my reputation." She shuddered and dropped her gaze. "I don't need people thinking they can comment on any part of my life. You pursuing whatever this is has their focus on me again."

"Because of Dave?"

Pain darkened her eyes, and he thrust his twitching hands into his pockets. He hadn't meant to hurt her, and now all he wanted to do was to hold her.

She jerked, backed up, and gestured him to enter. "What do you know about Dave?"

Slipping through the opening, he tried to act casual, like nothing momentous had happened. When inside, his heart tumbled and leaped, tossing fireflies into the pit of his stomach.

"Just what I overheard at Mindy's."

She sat in a brocaded antique high-back, her posture stiff, her ankles crossed as if she dined with royalty. "The pitying glances and hushed whispers hurt more."

"Why stay here?" He sat on the edge of an uncomfortable chaise longue, clasping his hands between his splayed knees.

"It's my home, and most folks are well-meaning. I didn't need it then, though." She pursed her lips. "Now, what do you want to apologize for, or was that an excuse?"

"For tonight. I'm sorry. Seeing you stripped me of my thoughts, my glib tongue." He'd been an unmitigated ass. "My intentions evaporated. I wanted you beneath me, and I reverted to caveman antics." He studied her flittering expressions, trying to gauge how she felt about his weak apology. In a way, it sounded as if he blamed her for his behavior. He sucked in a deep breath and leaped to his feet. "You were...are beautiful. I'm not blaming your dress, your sexy lips, fuck, even your alluring eyes. This was on me, all of it."

She nodded, a smile curling her plump lips. "So, you'll stop harassing me?"

He sat again, staring at her as he assessed what walking away from her felt like. Did he want to? No, nor did he want to never see her again. He wanted to know where this attraction led, why it was this intense, and why she mattered to him. She had the right to distrust his motives. They were strangers.

"I can't." He rubbed his palms along his thighs to his knees. As she trailed this action with her gaze, her mouth parted ever so slightly. She *was* attracted to him, and he could work on that. He needed to be in top form to seduce her. "Sitting here and not touching you is killing me."

"Does any woman say no to you?" Her voice was breathless, and she pressed the tip of her tongue onto her upper lip. She huffed. "There's no future for us, Tom."

Future? He struggled with now. The future could damn well wait.

"Dinner? This time away from prying eyes?" He grinned. "If you're going to bless me with another fake orgasm, I'd like for all of Gainsford not to share in the experience."

Pink splashed across her cheeks and traveled down her throat. A slow smile crawled across her lips, and she chuckled, bouncing her breasts. "The library is the most private."

He wanted to leap into the air and roar his victory. Gripping his knees, he restrained himself and cleared his throat. "Tomorrow night?" He had to be cool, calm, suave. He couldn't reveal how he ached to push her down onto her Persian rug and fuck her, covering each other with carpet burns as the fire warmed their writhing bodies.

"On one condition." She arched a dark-auburn brow. "If you mess this up, Bradshaw, you'll admit we're wrong and stop this." She gestured to the space between them with the flick of her finger.

Ice filled his chest, climbing from his gut to encase his heart. He didn't like this and didn't want to agree to it. "How about we visit Gram if I fail, and let her decide?"

She gaped. "She knows?" She threw up her palms. "Never mind. A full-grown man asking his grandmother for dating advice?"

"I respect her, value her opinion, and I'm too deep in this, too invested. She'll guide me with a fresh perspective." He scowled. Did she imply he couldn't date a girl without asking for the all-clear? His nostrils flared, and the urge to swat her backside made him jump up to pace. "Like you would ask Liz."

"Um, Tom…" She rose, crowding him as he wore a path in her rug, bringing with her a subtle floral fragrance. "We're not in a relationship, and I don't think we need couple's counseling." She pinched her brow. "Let's just do this thing tomorrow, and you'll see."

He cupped her elbows, and her warm softness reached his palms through the thin robe. He ran his hands up and down her upper arms, wanting to yank her closer but needing her to trust him. Her breathing stilled, and she trembled. She splayed her fingers across his pecs, but he wasn't sure she wanted to pull him closer or push him away. Trust had to be the starting point.

"What time?" He trailed his gaze over her upturned face. She wore no make-up, wasn't self-conscious about it, and the splattering of pale freckles on her cheeks was like discovering the lost jewel of Osiris.

"The fair ends at two, and the sun sets around five. How about six?" Uncertainty laced with vulnerability furrowed her brow, and he succumbed, pressing his lips to her temple. His breath hitched, and he tightened his fingers around her arms.

Pulling away, he smiled and tucked a curl behind her ear. "Six it is, Amelia." He strode toward the sliding door, opened it, then paused. "Thank you for speaking to me, and…good night."

She closed and locked the door behind him. Cold air hit him in the face, and he relished it, needing its calming effect. His cock ached, hard, eager, and evident in his loose jogging shorts. Conscious that she watched, he walked around her house and dived into the shadows.

Peeking around the wall, he watched as she put out the fire, her form revealed by the flickering flames. He sucked in a sharp breath, digging his fingertips into the siding. Served him right for spying. He spun on his heel and headed for the bed-and-breakfast, planning on a shower and a hand job. Now that she'd granted him another chance, blessed sleep should follow.

Chapter Nine

Did crazy people know they'd lost their minds? Amy was in the grip of madness. To agree to another date but in private? Yup, insanity. Seeing his face through the glass startled a scream, then slumped her shoulders in relief. He gained entry into her home because of Maude, and he swindled another date from her because of the intensity in his gaze. It verified every sinfully wicked word he said.

No man had ever spoken to her like that, as if the curve of her cheek and the shape of her breasts tormented him. Then he'd kissed her brow, nothing more despite the hard-on he sported. The ache that pulsed through her wanted more, needing him to bring those lips to hers. Said longing had kept her up, tossing, turning, and thumping her pillow.

The paraphernalia in her closet had brought her some relief, but it was shallow, lacking the wow factor of a real man. There weren't gasps and shudders, simply a predetermined path from A to B with the result a lackluster orgasm.

After an as disappointing night sleep, at the fair she stood. A sweet smile hopefully hid her troubled thoughts. With sweat trickling down her cleavage, she watched the rows of customers outside the age-defined kissing booths. She walked a fine line between spinster-Amy and closet-Amy. If she chose to let Tom have his way with her, and he would, if given a chance, what awaited her in the aftermath? Nothing stayed a secret.

Their cars outside the library or her home would raise suspicions.

"It's almost time to close." Sonja scanned the dwindling lines, her brown pixie hair styled in a mohawk. She'd married her high school sweetheart, had the two-point-five kids, picket fence, and perfect life. It was enough to bring tears to Amy's eyes.

"I'll head off any hopefuls." Amy hurried off the stand, past the waiting crowds to stand guard.

They'd done well today. She'd organized fifteen-year-old Felicity for the teens, Celeste for the adults, and effervescent Elise for the mature age range. If requested, handsome and charming Denver, the high school football captain sprawled on a chair against the backboard. Alongside him was Benson, the local fireman hero with a vest molding his chest muscles. Rumor had it, he and Celeste had an on-again-off-again thing going, and by the lingering gazes cast between them, that rumor was true. Elise's husband, Stan, handled the elderly women, Maude being one of them.

"Aunty Amy." Kimmy barreled toward her, and she dropped to scoop her niece into her arms.

"Hello, pumpkin." Amy kissed her temple, the only clean part of her face before smiling at Dave. "Hi, where's Liz?"

He gestured behind him with his thumb. "Someone challenged her to a shootout." He grinned, softening his face with a boyish appeal.

Amy paused, expecting the usual lancing of pain through her heart, but it didn't come. Raising a dazed face to his, she grinned. "Oh, the fool. Lizzy's been shooting possums for decades."

"What has you in a good mood?" His wariness pinched her chest with guilt.

"Since I have you all to myself, I wanted to apologize for my behavior. You see, I was in love with you for a while, but you chose my sister." She laughed, giving Kimmy another kiss. Her chest swelled, and a sense of weightlessness made her giddy.

He jerked back, surprise twisting his handsome face. "I...didn't know."

Relief slumped her shoulders. It had been one of her biggest fears, that he'd known and laughed at how pathetic she was. "I shouldn't have taken my resentment out on you, and for that, I'm sorry."

"I thought you hated me." His voice was soft, and his blue gaze gentle. "I wasn't kidding when I told Liz you intimidate me. So confident, so organized. I felt...less with you."

"Well, you got the better sister." Amy thrust out her hand. "Shall we start again?"

He clasped her hand in his massive mitts, then yanked her into his arms, squashing Kimmy between them. "Hell, yes."

Unable to fend him off, Amy had to endure his hug. Thankfully, it was a short one. "My sarcasm might be a habit now, so if I revert to my old ways, set me straight."

"And how would I do that under your sister's watch? She berates me after every interaction with you." He winced.

"We'll use a secret word or phrase." Amy grinned. "Something so random she won't figure it out. Then again, we'll have to explain it to her, lest she think we've lost our minds."

"The phrase is…candy floss." Dave scooped his squirming daughter out of Amy's arms.

"Yes, please, Daddy."

Dave laughed and kissed Kimmy, spinning on the spot so she'd squeal. "I'll see you at the barbecue."

"Barbecue?" Amy groaned. "I forgot about it."

"What if I invited the man who's staring at you like you're a toffee apple?"

Tom? She gasped and scanned the crowds. The face of Phillipe came into focus. She laughed at her silly reaction. "Don't you dare. That's my next-door neighbor's son."

Dave pointed his chin at something behind her. "Then how about the man striding toward us with a ferocious glower?"

Amy wasn't falling for it a second time. "No, thanks, I'm fine. Need me to bring anything?" She frowned. Having gotten up early to roast a chicken and make potato salad for dinner in the library, she supposed she could sacrifice the salad.

"Dave, I presume?" Tom's baritone slid ice down her spine then set it on fire.

She gaped and faced him. Holy Tolkien, he looked edible in his jeans and a tight green T-shirt. His ebony hair was damp and curled over his collar, and a shadow covered his jaw. She drew in a deep breath, searching for his cologne, then sighed when it filled her lungs.

"Dave, this is Tom Bradshaw." Her voice came out a little strangled, breathless. She clasped her hands before her, digging her nails into her skin. *Get a grip.* He wanted sex from her, nothing more. Sure, his sexual magnetism was off the charts, but the results would be the same—a broken heart.

Tom thrust out his hand, and at the same time, looped his arm around her waist, tugging her against his body. What was he doing? Furtive glances proved they were drawing attention. With a muffled groan, she tried to shuffle away, but he tightened his hold. Damn, if she didn't find his forcefulness panty-damping and breathtaking.

Dave was all smiles. "Nice to meet you, Tom. Interested in coming over for a barbecue?"

"If Amelia doesn't mind?" Tom captured her chin and raised her gaze to his. His focus lowered to her lips, tempting her to reciprocate.

Instead, she forced a huff. "Um, I feel like the two of you are bulldozing me."

"I'd love to come, but I'll need to leave by five. I have to be somewhere at six." He caressed his thumb across her bottom lip. "I can't miss it and don't want to."

Her tongue tied, and she nodded, drowning in the intensity of his eyes.

"Then it's settled." Dave studied the dwindling crowds. "Off to rescue Liz. See you two later."

Kimmy waved then clung to her father's shoulder with her tiny hands.

Amy waved back, blowing her niece kisses. "Sorry about that. You can pull out. I'll make an excuse."

Tom circled his other arm around her and pressed her against the length of him again. "You should know upfront, Amelia Perkins, that I don't *pull out.*"

Despite loving gripping his biceps, people were staring. She wiggled, trying to break his hold. "As innuendos go, that one's corny." When he continued to hold her, she stilled. Fine, time for reverse psychology. She plastered her body to his, making sure he felt every curve. "Tom Bradshaw." She lowered her voice, curling his name off her tongue as if she'd prefer to twirl her mouth around a certain part of his anatomy.

His breath hitched, and the green in his eyes darkened.

"Release me, or so help me, I'll knee you in the balls."

He chuckled and unfolded his arms, holding up his palms as if he was innocent.

She stomped off, heading to the kissing booth. "Last call, folks."

"One hundred to kiss Ms. Perkins," he called.

The crowd cheered, smothering her strangled cry.

She faced Tom, the height of the stand elevated her, giving her a false sense of bravado. "Two hundred to *not* kiss Mr. Bradshaw." She smirked, folding her arms across her chest.

The crowd laughed, a few encouraging him to up his price.

"One thousand." He loped up the steps and paused in front of her. "Another for the library."

She gaped, pinned to the spot by his generosity and the urgings of the crowd, Sonja among them.

He gathered her close, assuming her silence as agreement. She placed her palms on his pecs, planning on pushing him away if he crossed the line. He cupped her face, holding her in place as he trailed his gaze across her eyes, along her nose, and down to her lips. Then, with excruciating slowness, he descended, his gaze meeting hers, challenging her to pull away.

She held herself rigid, letting him have this one kiss. Not that she hadn't wanted him to kiss her. Holy Whitman, she fantasized about it, what he would taste like, how skillful his tongue might be.

He paused an inch from her lips, the heat of his mint breath warming her.

She trembled, kneading his chest, then stopped when she realized what she was doing. Her insides exploded, as if time passed but didn't, as if her heartbeat sought to align with his.

He glided his hands from her hips to under her arms, brushing a breast on the side away from onlookers. She gasped, her nipples puckering, then he swooped in, slanting his mouth across hers, his tongue slipping between her lips.

His groan vibrated down her throat.

Her heart stilled at the softness of his lips and the heat of his mouth. He dominated her, not with force, or his strength of will but by the subtle flicks of his tongue, the thrust and retreat until her knees trembled.

She moaned, tilted her head, and looped her arms around his neck. He'd paid for this kiss, and had she known he'd be this good, she might have let him kiss her for free.

Her mind snagged on the word, 'Paid.'

She pushed away, breaking contact, and sucked in deep breaths. With her hand on her heaving chest, she blinked at him. Wishing they were alone warred with her wish that he hadn't kissed her. It didn't help her sanity when she knew what he could do with his lips.

His posture was stiff, and his jaw clenched when he raised his fingers to brush a curl off her cheek. His nostrils flared as he snared her gaze. Something intense poured from him, but she couldn't name it.

"I'll wait by your car." He spun on his heel and jogged away, leaving her standing alone, a victim to the curious onlookers.

The crowd broke into applause. She ignored them, staring after Tom. Her lips tingled, and the addictive taste of his mouth lingered.

"Wow, who was that?" Sonja nudged her out of her lust-filled daze.

"Maude's grandson." Amy cleared her throat and faced the kissing booths. She gave her usual speech, thanking the volunteers and those willing to donate to their cause. This year, all proceeds went to the pediatric ward at Gainsford Memorial Hospital.

A team would dismantle the stands, and Sonja handled the tickets, leaving Amy to wander to her car. Dread or excitement shared the same sensations, a riot of butterflies that sent shivers through her body. She struggled to breathe, expecting to see Tom leaning against her teal convertible.

The parking lot had started to empty, and alongside her car stood his expensive silver BMW or Audi. They all looked the same to her, but it suited him as a banker. He leaned against the hood, his long legs crossed at the ankles.

The butterflies clawed their way up her throat. She offered her back to him, hoping he didn't notice her breathlessness and flushed cheeks. "You can follow me. It's not far."

His touch on her lower back made her jerk, and she faced him, startled again by how close he stood. She hadn't heard his footsteps.

"Let's leave my car here and go in yours. Less chance of anyone seeing me parked outside the library." He cupped her elbows, keeping her close. "Don't make me pay another thousand to kiss you, Amelia."

"Make you?" She gritted her teeth, fury firing her blood. Thumping him on the chest, she opened her door, forcing him back. "I didn't—"

"I would pay more for your sweet lips." If a mischievous smile didn't twitch his lips, she might have taken him seriously.

"Smooth talker, get in the car." She chuckled, admiring his graceful jog as he loped around the hood to slide in beside her. "I need to pick up a salad from home."

"What about a bottle of wine...or sherry?" He winked.

She stared at him, at his dimple. Shaking her head, she huffed, turned the ignition, and reversed the car, all under his watchful gaze. When he dropped his hand on her thigh, just above her knee, she yelped. A dart of lust shot to her aching core, and his touch burned her through her denim capris. She swatted his hand, but he tightened his grip.

"You're taking chances, Tom Bradshaw."

"Sue me, Amelia Perkins."

Chapter Ten

DAVE POINTED HIS BEER at Tom. "Your intentions better be honorable. I invited you because of how you look at her." He glanced at the kitchen window, checking to see if Amelia and Liz could hear him. Then swung his gaze to Kimmy at the swings.

Tom sighed. He'd taken one look at Dave hugging Amelia, and red had blurred his vision with fury pulsing along his veins. First The Rose Garden's bartender and now her brother-in-law? Tom blamed the volatile emotions she invoked in him, and perhaps, he'd continue on this jealous path until he'd fucked her. He pursed his lips and furrowed his brow. Maybe he'd be this way until he had her beneath him more than once.

"She's being stubborn." He sipped his beer, wishing it was something stronger.

Dave chuckled. "Yup, runs in the family." He flipped the steak over. "I'll see what I can do."

Tom jerked back. He didn't need help and certainly not from the man Amelia thought she'd been in love with.

"A little quiet time? Say a trip to the basement for Kimmy's jacket?" Dave laughed, oblivious to Tom's opinion. Although, time alone with her would be wonderful. "How long are you staying?"

The change of subject heralded the arrival of the women, bearing salads and rolls. They chatted as they laid the table, groaning under the amount of food. Amelia popped a soda and chose a chair beside Tom. He flicked his gaze at the can and shifted on his chair, trying to ease the renewed throbbing.

She'd tasted of cherry when he'd kissed her. That wasn't a flavor he was partial to but on her tongue... He downed his beer and crushed the can in his hand to vent his frustration. Popping a cherry soda for himself, he swirled the cold sweetness to coat every inch of his mouth.

As substitutes went, it was a pathetic one. Dinner tonight meant one thing in his mind, and he hoped she agreed. She'd kissed him as if they were alone, as if she yearned for him as much as he did for her. Yes, he'd take Dave up on his offer. A reminder might solidify their attraction.

"Comfortable?" He stared at her blue toenails; her feet bare. She'd discarded her shoes the moment she'd entered the house. Without analyzing the urge, he placed his can beside the chair and scooped her foot onto his lap. She resisted until he ran his thumb along her instep. Her mouth parted on a deep groan.

Fuck.

With her heavy-lidded gaze and those lips he longed to taste again, she was a sex goddess enticing him to his doom.

"I don't let anyone touch my feet," she rasped.

He could understand why with the way his cock throbbed in reaction. As he continued to massage her feet, her demeanor softened, her body language opened up, and she let him into her world. The sexual tension was there, but now she laughed and teased him, almost as if she'd lowered her guard.

This woman was breath-taking. He split his focus between Dave and Liz. Hands down, Tom would have chosen Amelia. Liz was lovely, he had no doubt, but Amelia's sensuality hummed desire through his body. She didn't try to seduce him, and for that, he was grateful.

Her fake orgasm last night had been torturous yet delicious to endure.

The afternoon passed like he was with Callum and Chrissy. He could be himself, with no one judging his reactions or comments. His lunch partner was adorable Kimmy, who shared her hot dog with him, her ice cream, and candy. The child was sweet, well-behaved, but as the hours ticked past, her energy waned.

"Amy, please would you fetch Kimmy's jacket from the toy room." Dave scooped his sleepy daughter off Tom's lap with a wink.

Amelia leaped to the task, putting her soda on the table as she barreled into the house. Bats exploded in Tom's stomach while he watched her disappear. Should he take Dave up on this offer?

"Dang, I forgot to ask for the purple jacket? Tom, would you mind?"

Liz frowned at Dave. "She doesn't have—"

"Sure." Tom chuckled, hurrying into the cool shadows of the house, ignoring their whispered argument. He paused outside the open basement door, drew in a deep breath, and climbed down the stairs, stopping to bolt the door closed behind him.

The basement was an open-plan toy room with a guest bedroom and en suite bathroom to the rear.

"Which jacket?" Amelia's voice crackled the baby monitor.

With a flick of his thumb, he switched that off. He behaved like a predator, navigating the hazards of a toy jungle, his focus on his prey, who sifted through a pile of folded laundry.

"Dave said the purple one."

She squeaked and faced him, two jackets in her hands. Her grip tightened, and her lips pursed. She must have sensed his prowling because she trembled.

He tugged the jackets out of her hands and tossed them onto the couch. Then he gripped her hips and pulled her closer to him.

"Wh-what are you doing?" She splayed her hands on his chest.

"Trying to resist temptation and failing." Unable to fight it any longer, he caressed his lips across hers, her sweet cherry-flavored breath calling to him. He'd swear before a panel of peers how his knees weakened, how his mind refused to focus on a thought. Driven mad by a woman too sexy for words, he was in a quagmire of lust.

"Taking liberties?" Fear skittered across her eyes, and he stilled.

She was trying to be tough, to fight this attraction, as if she expected him to break her heart. That moment of vulnerability she revealed to him, strengthened his control. He had no intention of hurting her; she had to know this.

"Repaying the favor," he forced a smile, but his heart twanged.

"What—?"

He captured her soft lips against his, lashing his tongue across hers. She groaned, and her fingers kneaded his chest as she'd done at the kissing booth. Desperate to feel every curve, he crushed her against him. He loved the taste of her, adored kissing her, and cherished each flick of her tongue. She wasn't a victim of their attraction, she participated, reciprocated, and desired him as much as he wanted her.

Spinning her until her back pressed along his chest, he tilted her head to capture her lips again. With seeking fingers, he unzipped her jeans. She gasped, and he deepened the kiss, teasing her until she forgot about him gripping her zipper open.

He slipped his hand inside, and she squirmed, rubbing her backside across his erection. His eyes fluttered shut against the sweet, heated sensations burning and bombarding him. With a shift of his hand, her breast filled his palm. He kneaded it while he sought entry with his fingers between her thighs. She wore something lacy that didn't hinder his intrusion.

As he rubbed his forefinger along her damp seam, her sweet whimper inflamed him, her nails digging into his forearms. The sharp darts of pain did nothing to diminish the lust pounding at him. He slid his fingers between her lips and paused on her nub, choosing that moment to focus on twirling his tongue around hers.

Her breath hitched, and she shivered in his arms. That wasn't an act. She was a real woman in the throes of passion. There weren't hidden motives, and her desire had nothing to do with his wealth and prestige. She was a woman who wanted him, his touch.

He opened his eyes to watch the pink splashing her cheeks, the flutter of her eyelashes on her freckled skin as he twirled his finger around her nub. She quivered, moans peppering the thrust of her tongue, and the grinding of her ass against his cock.

He shuddered, wishing he could yank her jeans down and bury himself in her. But no, this was a matter of trust, and he owed her a real orgasm. Expecting Liz to bang on the basement door, he increased his speed, tormenting Amelia until her breathing scattered, and her body writhed beyond her control.

He adored every reaction—a sigh, gasp, or shudder, but what tore through him was her moans and whimpers.

She was close.

Chapter Eleven

AMY WOULD KILL TOM if he stopped now. Seeing him standing there with her alone in the basement had sent shivers of anticipation through her body. He'd prowled around her with graceful movements, his gaze on nothing else but her. Then he'd kissed her, and her resistance crumbled.

Not that she'd been strong to begin with. From the second he'd clasped her elbows in the library, she'd fought a losing battle. Now, with his mouth on hers, his tongue flicking hers, and his fingers between her thighs, she couldn't think of a reason not to let him have his way with her.

Waves of heated pleasure pulsed outward, and the throb grew, intensifying until she ached. Nothing she did eased the need burning in her core and wherever he touched her. She broke the kiss to arch her back, resting her head on his shoulder. With one hand tweaking her nipple and the rough pad of his thumb punishing her nub, she whimpered, moaned, and gasped like a practiced courtesan.

She didn't care. It felt too good, sinful, delicious, and decadent, as if her entire existence had waited for this moment. Tingles spread outward and inward, and she clawed her way up the ecstasy mountain, teetering on the edge.

"Kiss me, Amelia."

She tilted her head and obeyed, just as he pinched her nub, plummeting her over the edge. Pleasure danced and skittered along her nerves. Screaming into his mouth, she shuddered against his unceasing onslaught as her ability to breathe escaped her, and her body turned into soft licorice.

He spun her in his arms again and kissed her.

Physics 530, he owned her, every nerve in her body, every sense available to her. She clung to him as if he were hers to keep, as if they'd been lovers for years. He pulled away to fix her zipper, tuck in her shirt, and fluff her hair.

She stood there, her body humming, and her mind still missing its ability to think.

"Amelia?" His deep tenor reverberated through her, and she smiled.

"Ah-ha," she mumbled, licking her lips.

"You're dropping me off at my car, I'm heading back to the bed-and-breakfast. I'll jog to your home and fuck you until dawn." He cupped her face, forcing her to meet his stormy-hazel gaze. "Got a problem with that?"

A small voice warned her that she was stronger than this, but the ecstasy in her veins silenced the negativity. She shook her head.

His shoulders slumped, and he grinned. There was beauty in his curling lips and dimpling cheek. "Good."

"Repaying what favor?" He'd said that, right? Something about a favor? As the lassitude drained from her, her cheeks flushed hot then cold. Had she let him kiss and touch her? Her sensitive core twanged, and she squirmed. He'd touched her intimately, and damn Darwin, she craved more.

"An orgasm for an orgasm." Before she could respond, he kissed her again, sliding his arms around her to trap her against him.

Tolkien have mercy, she loved his kisses and how they made her feel. Excitement, desire, anticipation exploded in her, and she kissed him back. His groan in reaction urged her on. He made her feel desirable, and for that, she'd succumb. After all, that's what a woman wanted. Desirability, appreciation, and occasionally, a little worshipping.

His lips were soft, his tongue spicy and hot, and he wielded it with such expertise. Shivers rippled along her body when he nibbled on her lips then kissed the bruised flesh. His heavy breathing and the thumping of his heart proved he wasn't faking his desire.

She didn't want to be anyone's passing fancy.

Lacing his fingers through hers, he tugged her out of the basement. Only Dave was in the garden, so she excused herself, desperate for a little space, to breathe, to think, and perhaps, in the quiet of the passage, to squeal like a teenager.

"There you are." Liz popped her head through the kitchen door. "Did you find Kimmy's purple jacket?

Heat scorched Amy's cheeks. "No, I only found a pink and a blue one."

Liz dipped her chin to her chest, trying to hide her laughter.

Amy paused, suspicion coiling around her spine. "Spill it, Elizabeth Coleman." She dropped her hands on her hips, just as their mother did.

"Kimmy doesn't have a purple jacket, but your truce with Dave has him playing matchmaker."

"Matchmaker?" Amy gasped, slumping against the door frame. "In what way?" He sent her to fetch the jacket, the conniving, two-faced...traitor. "I could kick his as...donkey." She sliced a glance at Kimmy to confirm she hadn't heard Amy's almost-slip. "Do you think Tom was part of it?"

Cold slithered down her back, collided with her lust-heated core, and fizzled out. Had he planned this? She shook her head, not wanting to believe it. If he did, what did it matter? He hadn't lied about his lewd intentions.

Then again, their recent interaction might be coloring her opinion of him. Just like that, with one orgasm, she was ready to spread her legs. She pressed her fingers to her cheeks.

"I've never seen a more determined man. Like I said, test him out, sis." Liz chuckled. "So, who chose candy floss?"

Amy shrugged, trailing Liz into the kitchen when Kimmy darted outside. "Dave did. So far, he's had to use it twice. I am trying, though."

"And I love you for it." Liz packed away the remnants of the green salad into the fridge. "Sorry about last night."

Stiffening her shoulders, Amy pushed off the counter. "Yes, well, it was a disaster."

Liz's laughter bobbed the knife, so she put it down. "I heard. The poor man, Amy. Show him some kindness. They say it was worse than Niles's date."

Amy huffed. Kindness? Letting Tom shove his fingers down her jeans? She was the kindest woman in Gainsford. "Neither were dates, Liz."

"Tom could've been. Just charm him if you want to keep him." She took up the knife again to slice lemon for iced tea. "You're scared, and I get that, but nothing worth it in this life comes without a price. Give a little."

"If I do, and he scurries back to Anham, do I get an I-told-you-so?"

Liz pointed the knife at Amy. "There you go, so pessimistic."

"Amelia?" Tom's voice traveled along the passage.

Amy stiffened and popped her head through the kitchen door like Liz had done. She gaped at him, heat scorching her cheeks anew. This man had kissed her, touched her, and despite wanting him to do it again, she couldn't believe how wanton she'd behaved.

He strolled along the passage, a sweet smile curling his lips, and her gaze dipped to his low-riding jeans. "Ready to go?"

She nodded, not trusting her voice when he crowded her to let Dave pass him in the narrow passage. Tom's fingers at her elbows skittered excitement along her arms to her nipples and the nape of her neck. She dipped her chin to hide her awe. Just... Wow.

With Kimmy playing, saying goodbye was without fuss, and soon, Amy reversed her car out of the driveway. Arm-in-arm, Dave and Liz waved, but silence thickened the tension between Amy and Tom.

He stretched his arm along the back of the seat and turned his body to watch her.

She snuck glances at him, a self-conscious smile teasing her lips. "What?"

He caressed her neck, sending heat outward. His touch was so feather-soft yet lethal to her senses. She gripped the steering wheel, hoping to hide her trembling from him, not needing to inflame his ego.

"Just looking at you, Amelia." His voice deepened as if he knew of her weakness for his baritone.

She smothered a snort, choosing to purse her lips against spewing something sarcastic. Just looking at her, like he was contemplating sampling the goods. She doubted he'd spend much time admiring her after he'd taken his fill. Sexual anticipation was like beer, too much of it, and everyone looked pretty.

She pulled alongside his silver toy car, and he hopped out. He looped around the hood and paused beside her door.

"I'd kiss you here and now, but I doubt you'd let me." He chuckled, tucking a curl behind her ear and tracing his finger along her jaw. "See you at sunset." Raising his gaze to the peach and purple sky, he nodded. "Soon."

She waved as if this was goodbye when inside, her stomach twisted into a hot mess. Holy Whitman, she needed to hurry home to bath and to tidy her bedroom, perhaps throw on fresh sheets. The aroma of roast chicken still filled her house, and a roaring fire wouldn't be a miss.

This was not what she'd planned for the evening. A quiet meal in the library and a final farewell to Tom, but now, she wanted to pamper herself, to prepare for what the night promised.

Her breath caught, and she pressed on the gas, needing to make it home with every spare minute precious. She opened the garage door as she pulled into her driveway, parked her teal baby, and leaped out before the engine switched off completely.

Slamming her front door shut behind her, she inhaled roast chicken and grimaced. She darted around, opening every window and the sliding door before lighting scented candles. While a fire flickered in the hearth, she made her bed with fresh sheets, choosing muted colors like cream and white. Chuckling, she imagined his face if she went full-floral with stuffed teddies overflowing her bed and shelves.

Sweat slicked her cleavage, and she frowned at the clock. Within minutes, she had her tub filling, her nightgown laid out, and the fragrance of honeysuckle filling the bathroom. If she hurried, she could wash, dress, and sip sherry in the lounge before he arrived.

Should she shave?

Grabbing her razor, she cursed under her breath.

Chapter Twelve

The sliding door was open, sweet Ella Fitzgerald crooned in the background, and the subtle fragrance of vanilla tickled Tom's nose. He slid the door closed, locking it, not needing accidental intrusions. He wanted Amelia to himself.

She wasn't at her desk, so he toed off his sneakers and pulled off his socks. As he crept down the passage, he wondered how he'd feel if he found her sprawled on her bed in one of her vintage nightgowns. His heart leaped, and he released a shuddering breath.

"Amelia?" He kept his voice low, not risking her neighbor hearing him through the lull between Ella songs.

No response came so he pushed her bedroom door fully open. There! On the bed lay something black and seductive with Amelia absent. He frowned. She wouldn't run, and it wasn't in her to hide.

Her bedroom was simple, in monochromatic colors. Mirrored doors lined one wall, which he assumed held her clothing. There wasn't a closet that screamed 'mysterious.' Perhaps it was somewhere else in her home. He pursed his lips, extending his fingers to clasp the handle of the only door leading off her room.

"...fish are jumping and the cotton..." A splash smothered her voice.

He grinned, pushing the door open to lean his shoulder on the frame.

In a claw-foot tub, with soap gliding down her bare back, and her arms raised to wash her hair, sat the woman of his erotic fantasies. She hummed, swirling her shoulders to the music, threatening to lift her breasts above the bubbles.

The heat of the room slapped his cheeks, and his breath came in huffs. Her tormenting scent saturated the air. Now he knew how it perfumed her skin. She slid deeper to rinse her hair, thrusting her knees up. The water threatened to spill over the edge.

With her eyes closed, she lay there, her face and breasts the only peach among the fading bubbles. She lifted a foot, catching the plug's chain with her toes. Yet, she didn't rise, continuing to lay there as the water drained, exposing her enticing curves inch by inch. He settled his gaze on the dark dusky nipples puckering now they weren't submerged.

His mouth watered. Fuck, he'd never seen anything so captivating.

He pushed off the door frame and leaned over the tub to grip the sides. Then, without touching any other part of her, he brushed his mouth across hers.

Her eyelids flew open on a gasp. Her cheeks darkened in an instant. He didn't move back so she could sit up. Instead, he ran the tip of his tongue along her bottom lip. Moaning, he dipped into her mouth, a groan tearing from him at her sherry flavor enhancing her natural sweetness.

He pressed his fingertips against the tub, tightening his hold. Not touching her added to the anticipation, but he didn't need it, not with the burning ache in his throbbing cock. Still, he persevered, loving that only his lips received the pleasure of hers.

The gurgle of the water as it drained drew him out of his mesmerized state. He pulled away. She shivered, goosebumps rippling across her pale skin. Her wet hair, dark against her skin, pooled around her, trailing her when he lifted her out of the bathtub. She squeaked, but he ignored her, crowding her as he flexed his fingers at her waist.

He dropped his gaze to the agitated rise and fall of her breasts, water rivulets dripping onto the fluffy rug beneath her feet.

"Fuck," he growled, caressing her arms to her shoulders then her neck to bury his fingers in her wet hair. Her skin was heated silk, and her shivering echoed the tremble in his weakening knees.

"Tom...um, how...?" She shuffled back, twisting to yank a towel off its rail to wrap around her. "You're early." She folded her arms across her knotted towel.

"If I didn't need a shower, you'd be beneath me now, Amelia."

Her breath hitched while she studied his face for a few seconds. She pinched her lips then nodded. "The guest bedroom has an en suite. You can find it yourself." With a huff, she spun on her heel and stomped out of the bathroom.

He frowned. Was she upset that he'd entered her home without knocking? Or that he'd intruded on her bathing? He trailed her into her room but stilled, blood rushing his face before pooling in his loins. She'd whipped off the towel and bent over to wrap it around her head, flaunting the enticing curve of her ass. Then with angry movements, she tugged on a black sheer nightgown with spaghetti straps before storming down the passage.

Fuck, Amelia naked was…breathtaking. Her skin glowed from the hot bath, and her eyes glittered with a mixture of fury and vulnerability.

He followed, pausing by a door he assumed had to be the guest bedroom. Opening it confirmed his assumption, and he yanked off his tank, tossing it onto the bed. Within minutes, he climbed out of the shower, wrapped a towel around his hips, and went in search of his prey. Her vulnerability might mean he'd startled or worse, frightened her, which hadn't been his intention. The opened door had led him to believe she waited for him. In his dazed lust, he hadn't given it deeper thought.

In silence, Amelia sat in her antique single chair, her legs crossed at the knees and a full glass of sherry clasped in her fingers. Her nightgown draped over her nipples and pooled on her lap, hiding her sex but exposing her bare legs. His fingers twitched to touch her.

"I'm sorry, I didn't mean to frighten you," he said.

She jerked back, and her mouth parted. Whatever she was about to say, she must have thought better of it. Shaking her head unraveled the towel. She yanked it off but gripped it on her lap.

With a gentle tug, he slipped it out of her hands and draped it across a nearby stool. He lifted the glass from her fingers and sipped from it, swirling the tart flavor across his tongue. Placing the glass on the kitchen counter, he kneeled in front of her, shuffling forward until he gripped her knees.

She sucked in a sharp breath, stiffening her legs before succumbing to the gentle pressure of his thumbs. She spread her thighs, granting him access to slip his hips between them.

He fought the urge to roar in triumph as he caressed her smooth thighs before burying his fingers beneath her ass. There, he gripped her cheeks, yanking her closer until her sex rubbed across his aching cock through the towel. He hissed, closing his eyes to calm his clamoring instincts. Not wanting to rush this moment *and* wanting to savor her reactions, he focused on his next move, nothing further.

His body didn't agree. His fingers massaged her flesh filling his palms. His heart thumped a rhythm without a melody, and his lungs squeezed the air out before it could replenish the oxygen in his veins.

He dipped his head and buried his face in the curve of her neck, kissing the pulse there. She trembled then scraped her fingernails along his forearms, as if she tested the texture of his skin. She squirmed in the chair, the action screaming her rising need.

He dusted kisses up her neck until he could nip her ear. At her whimper, he aimed for her lips, rubbing his across hers, consuming her breaths, and fighting the lure of her hot tongue. Groaning, he caved, delving into her mouth. Sheer bliss engulfed him. There was nowhere else he wanted to be.

~*~

Tom gyrated his hips, brushing his hard-on where Amy needed it the most. She struggled to hold onto her anger. Fear had shot through her when he'd kissed her, trapping her in the bathtub. Then his reaction had scattered her thoughts despite the staccato of her heartbeat reminding her she'd been scared a moment ago. She *had* left the sliding door open, but she'd thought she still had time to bathe, dress, and await him.

His fingers dug into her backside cheeks, kneading. The action tugged on her core, shooting pangs of need that snatched her ability to breathe. With his mouth on her throat, his teeth at her ear, and his lips feathering across hers, she quivered. Shards of bold, breathless lust bolted from her nipples to her sex. She murmured a 'yes.'

Brushing her nails through the hair on his forearms only intensified her longing to splay her fingers across his damp chest. Holy Whitman, in a towel he was awe-inspiring, sculpted caramel, contoured edges, and steam from his shower poured off him. His damp hair curled where his neck met his shoulders, but his hazel gaze ensnared her. His eyes were darker, intense, with his focus on her predatorial.

She didn't stand a chance. When he'd gripped her knees, then with gentle pressure parted her thighs, her heart had thumped out a Rammstein rhythm, and hot, coiling need had consumed her belly.

Despite the trembling, she wanted more, now. She licked his bottom lip, longing to kiss him, aching for his tongue to dominate her.

"Amelia, please, touch me." He gathered her hands to his chest. Arching his back, he closed his eyes on a low moan.

She splayed out her fingers, testing the texture of his firm, heated muscles. Dipping her head, she caught a droplet, tasting his skin. The salty flavor of him was, in an instant, addictive. His breath hitched, encouraging her boldness. She sipped stray droplets, nipping then kissing before wrapping her mouth around a taut nipple. He shivered, a growl vibrating his chest under her lips.

Pushing her back, he looped his fingers under the nightgown's straps, gliding them off her shoulders before feathering his touch along the drooping neckline. With his pinky fingers, he dipped inside the nightgown, caressing her skin and areolas. Her breasts swelled, growing achingly heavy. She shuddered with tingles accompanying the puckering of her nipples.

He pinched one between his fingers through the fabric and drew a whimper from her. He rolled it across his palm before tugging gently. She cried out, arching her back to thrust her breast into his hand, needing his touch. Her other breast throbbed, as if jealous. Cupping it to appease it, she tested out pinching her nipple to compare to his touch.

"Amelia." His voice was rough, rubbing along her senses and sending shivers down her spine.

Then she was airborne, thrown over his shoulder. She squealed, gripping his waist, his skin hot under her fingers. He massaged her bared backside cheek, shooting more darts to her sex. She moaned, clenching her thighs together against the growing ache.

His towel slipped off as he carried her down the passage. She stared, not wanting to blink. He had a tight backside. Hesitating then succumbing, she ran a palm over one cheek. When he groaned, she squeezed it.

He dipped his fingers between her thighs, coming close to touching her where she burned for him. Her breath stilled in anticipation, but he tossed her onto her bed. Flicking her damp hair out her face, she stared. He stood there, one knee on her bed, his mouth parted as if he too couldn't breathe. His hard-on bobbed.

Gorgeous. Every delicious inch of him was something to admire. Hard edges, carved indents, velvet skin against his tousled ebony hair and appraising gaze. Her mouth dried, and her brain turned to mush. He crawled across the bed to her, resting his weight on his hands in a permanent push-up. His muscles rippled as he brought his face in line with hers.

"Ready for this, Amelia?"

She paused, understanding what he was asking. As aroused as he was, he offered her a chance to stop. This meant more to her than he could know. She nodded, not trusting her tongue to do anything besides lick her lips, his skin, and a certain part of his anatomy.

"Say it." His voice dipped low, just the way she liked it.

She swallowed. "Yes."

"Spread those thighs for me."

She obeyed without hesitation. His gaze settled on her sex, his jaw hardened, and a pulse ticked at the base. He sprawled alongside her, dropping a hand on her upper thigh. Rubbing his thumb, he relished the silkiness of her skin, then caressed his fingers up, over her hip and soft stomach, gathering the fabric with it. Her baby-doll nightgown gave him no resistance. When he cupped her breast, skin on skin, a tightness in her core began to build.

He claimed her mouth, thrusting in his tongue, flicking it across hers and along her lips before kissing her chin, her collarbone, and one nipple through the fabric. When he sucked it into his mouth, his hand trailed a fiery path down her belly. Rubbing the pad of his thumb along her seam had her crying out. She jerked, her hips rising, urging him onward.

He didn't, sucking on her nipple instead. She whispered his name, gripping her bedding as heat, ecstasy, yearning lanced from her nipple to her core. He toyed with her, twirling her nipple with his tongue, sucking before blowing across it. The chiffon didn't hinder him.

Then he kissed her again, and she responded, plunging her tongue in to duel with his, to learn every crevice of his mouth. Something tugged on her heart, but she ignored it. Through his tormenting kiss, he continued to stroke her seam, maintaining a slow, torturous rhythm. She was close to begging him to touch her, to ease the sharp darts of almost-painful longing.

He broke the kiss, his breathing coming in huffs, but he ensnared her gaze, as if he waited. The rubbing of his thumb across her nub spiked heated pleasure through her, thrumming her nerves, and she arched her back on a silent scream. Her shudder melted into a permanent tremble when he circled her tight bundle of nerves.

She stilled with each swirl of his finger, drawing a gasp from her. Intense, aching need gyrated her hips, and she released the bedding to grip his hand.

"What do you want, Amelia?" He pressed tiny kisses to her eyelids, cheek, and chin.

"You, Tom." She licked her bottom lip.

He caught her tongue in his mouth. At the same time, he thrust a finger inside her but swirled his thumb across her nub. It was too much, the intensity, the mind-blowing pleasure, his delicious mouth. She screamed, coming apart and uncaring that she twitched as she shattered. Tingles shot outward, inward, arching her off the bed.

The withdrawal of his fingers made her whimper. She was still sensitive, and the slightest touch sent mini quivers through her.

He sucked on his fingers, closing his eyes on a growl. "You're so fucking delicious." He bolted off the bed, returning a minute later with a stack of condoms. She rose onto her elbows to watch him, chuckling at his intention to use so many.

Dropping a packet at her hip, he settled between her thighs, gripping her hips to press an open-mouthed kiss to her belly. The nightgown had ridden up, and he tugged on it, peeling it off her with her help.

He leaned back to stare at her, his gaze a scorching path from breast to breast to her glistening sex. His nostrils flared, and he ran his thumb over her seam again. "I wanted you the moment we met."

He tore the wrapper open with his teeth, peeling the condom over his cock. She frowned, having wanted to run her tongue along the length of him.

"I wanted to fuck you bent over the check-in counter." He pressed his hard-on at her entrance and pushed in an inch at a time. She moaned, loving him stretching and filling her.

"You did?" She clung to his biceps, closing her eyes against the fresh wave of intense pleasure pulsing outward.

"I knew you'd feel like this." He released her hips, now that he was buried in her, to capture her lips with his. The taste of herself peppered his tongue as he dominated her mouth, skittering her heartbeat and stealing a little of her soul.

Then he withdrew and thrust in, balls deep. A feral groan tore from him.

Her voice lodged in her throat when pure ecstasy sparked along her nerve endings. She feathered her fingers along his shoulders to bury in his hair, scraping his scalp. With each thrust, each connection of his hips to hers, the merging of the fine sweat layering their bodies, and the sweet cacophony of their enjoyment, the pleasure grew. The intensity ramped, and the sheer beauty of it brought tears to her eyes. She screamed, shattering again, and he swallowed her cries, whimpers, and breathless moans with his kisses.

He didn't stop, his thrusts steady and deep, hitting all her points until she splintered again and again. Then with one final thrust, he stilled, his handsome features contorted as if he was in pain, and he grunted. He gripped her thighs, bruising her. His nipples puckered as he bent back, closed his eyes, and shuddered.

"Just like I imagined." He settled his gaze on her. "You're perfect, Amelia."

Warmth flooded her at his admiration, not that she'd done anything but lie there and take it. She trailed her fingers from his collarbone to his belly button, and he snatched her fingers, bringing them to his lips for a kiss.

"Later, I plan to do this again, just harder, faster." He grinned, faltering her breath with a dimpled cheek. "Rougher." His voice was hoarse as he said that.

She smiled. Delicious tendrils of freshly satiated desire rose inside her at his promise.

"I look forward to it." And she did. She'd just become his latest conquest, and at that moment, she didn't care.

Chapter Thirteen

AMELIA HAD SHUFFLED OFF the bed, heading to the kitchen for a bottle of water. Tom lay there, reeling, his body still thrumming from the best orgasm of his life. He frowned. Well, in the last ten years. He glanced at his cock, still hard, eager, which was, in itself, surprising. Had she aroused him so much he could go all night? He knew better.

"Hungry?" she called from the kitchen.

"I could eat." He rolled over and buried his face in her pillow, receiving a deep inhalation of fabric softener for his stupidity. What he'd hoped for was her scent, one that teased yet eluded his nostrils.

Something heavy pressed on his mind. He recognized it as tomorrow and the judgmental expectations of the future. He didn't want to dwell on it now, wanting to enjoy this time with her, instead.

With her breasts swaying, she staggered into her bedroom, carrying a picnic basket. Releasing a deep huff, she hoisted it onto the bed, opening the basket to pull out a blanket. He admired the play of light on her alabaster skin, the contrasting red of her hair, the dusk tones of her areolas, and the sweet noises she made as she worked.

Was she aware she pranced around in her nudity, his focus unerring? Then she dropped to the floor, folding her legs Indian-style, uncaring that she exposed her still-flushed sex to his hungry gaze.

"Roast chicken? Strawberries?" She wrapped her lush lips around the red fruit, and his cock twitched.

Bolting off the bed, he kneeled behind her, pulling her back against his thighs. He ran his palm from collarbone to her chin to tilt her head back. She peered at him, her parted lips luring him. He captured her mouth with his, needing to taste her and the tart strawberry. With a rumble of approval, he licked her lips, using his tongue to search for every morsel.

"You can have your own." Her smile was sensual and teasing despite her breathlessness.

He cupped her cheeks, holding her still for a long kiss, not understanding the tumultuous emotions bombarding his heart. Later, he would unravel everything she evoked. Sprawling alongside her on the blanket, he studied her from her mussed hair to her glistening sex.

He flitted his gaze to her lips when she sucked on her thumb. Her pink tongue wrapped around her finger, and a sharp pang of lust jabbed him in the groin.

He released a slow controlled breath and blinked at the food she placed before him: chicken, bowls of baby carrots, cherry tomatoes, miniature bread rolls, and an array of cheeses. She popped a tomato in her mouth, her lips twisting into a smile when she trailed a lingering gaze over his body.

"Not quite what I had in mind for the library," she said.

He chuckled, picking a piece of chicken to put on his plate. "Oh, this is infinitely better."

"You think?" Her good humor faded, and sadness darkened her eyes.

She shifted, folding an arm across her breasts to hide from him. He frowned, not liking this change in her like sex was something to be ashamed about.

One night jockey, she'd called him. Perhaps she feared more than one night? Or that tonight was it? He opened his mouth to ask but no words came to mind.

She rolled onto her stomach, resting on her elbows with her breasts cushioning her. Her feet kicked up, her toes curling as she shredded the strip of chicken with her fingers. The sadness didn't leave her eyes despite the trembling smile she offered him.

Without lying to her, he didn't know what to say. He was who he was—a career lawyer from the city and a serial womanizer. Having yet to weigh his options, he couldn't promise her a future. All he could assure her is that he wanted her. Once hadn't been enough.

"You're not eating." She pointed to his untouched food. Neither was she, the chicken shredded into thin strips.

Sipping from the bottle of water she'd given him, he ran his appraising gaze across her face, admiring the splatter of freckles on her cheeks. He closed the bottle, dropped it beside his plate, and lunged for her, capturing her chin between his forefinger and thumb.

The savory flavor of roast chicken glazed her lips, and the tartness of the tomato coated her tongue. Yet, beneath it was her essence, driving lust through him. It was this he searched for, trying to capture it with his mouth, his fingers threading her hair, his cock buried in her. No matter how much he tasted her, it wasn't enough—it didn't satiate this insane need.

He gathered her close, pulling her against his chest, crushing her until her soft warmth and sweet scent engulfed him. Beneath his knees, tomatoes and carrots tumbled out of their bowls, but he didn't care.

Pulling away to bury his face in her hair, he fought to breathe, to understand this obsession. "I promised you rough."

She gasped, and he swooped in to kiss her. He had planned on fucking her from behind, running the pads of his fingers over her curves. Yet, he hesitated. He didn't want to bruise her, even by accident.

Slipping his fingers between her thighs, he stroked her drenched sex. The vibration of her moans poured over his tongue, and he tightened his grip on her upper arm. She shuddered, gyrating her hips in alignment with his swirling thumb, and in the process, rubbed her puckered nipples across his chest.

Tingles shot up from his balls, and his cock dribbled. He wasn't going to last long if she kept reacting so fucking beautifully to his every touch. And where were the condoms? Too far away to help him now.

With a growl, he released her and lunged for the nightstand. He tore open the condom with his teeth and fumbled, his fingers slippery. She layered her hands over his, calming his frantic movements. Tossing the wrapper on the nightstand, she rolled the condom onto his aching cock.

He hissed when she rubbed the length of him, sliding and stroking in torturous slow motion. Then she laughed, then sucked on his nipple as she gave his erection one last pump.

"Witch," he said, gripping her upper arms to break the connection between the sweet heat of her mouth and his sensitive nipple. "On your knees, Amelia." His voice was hoarse, his words gravel and almost indiscernible.

She clambered onto the bed, arching her back as she pressed her forehead to the duvet.

Fuck. He'd never seen anything this sexy. He stroked an ass cheek, stroking the smooth skin with trembling fingers. Placing a knee on either side of hers, he positioned his cock at her channel. He slid in a little, just to ensure he had the right angle, then grabbed her hips.

With one thrust, he buried himself. She mewled, mauling the bed linen. Tiny sparks of joy skittered along his cock. He moaned, kneading the flesh at her hips. He gathered his dwindling control and pulled out, closing his eyes on the exquisite pleasure yet deep sense of loss that action invoked in him.

With another thrust, he was part of her, fused, one. He draped over her to cup her breast, pinching the nipple as he withdrew again, leaving the tip of his cock dipping into her entrance.

She whimpered, cried out, begged, and moaned, gyrating her ass until she ground against him. "Tom, harder, please, fuck me harder."

He doubted his hearing since she didn't swear.

"What do you want, sweetheart?" He grinned, sliding into her inch by inch then withdrawing his cock at a torturous pace.

"Tom Bradshaw, if you don't give me rough like you promised—"

He thrust into her, his hips hitting her ass, his balls slapping her sex. She screamed. Sweet waves of intense heat engulfed him. He groaned, pistoning in and out of her with so much force that she came again.

His cock was in agony. A tingling, aching need rippled from his balls to the tip, and with one final thrust, he roared. Darkness swirled his vision. Heated pleasure, contentment, a rightness with the world settled on him as he rode out tiny quivering aftershocks that flexed his fingers still cupping her breast.

He kissed her shoulder before collapsing on the bed, taking her with him. Not wanting to break the connection just yet, he stayed inside her. Their labored breathing filled the silence, and when she shivered in his arms, he reached across her to yank her duvet, tucking it around them.

He hooked her waist, just under her breasts, and pulled her snug against his chest. A fine sheen of sweat coated them, but he didn't care. He didn't want her to move, to sever this moment with reality.

"Did you swear?" He nudged curls aside to kiss her ear.

She mumbled something in her sleep and said no more.

Burying his nose in her hair, he tightened his arms but lay awake. For the first time in a long while, he was content.

Chapter Fourteen

AMY COULDN'T MOVE. HER wrapped duvet and Tom's chest at her back trapped her. The twitter of birds had woken her, but she snuggled into his embrace, savoring the final moments before they parted for good. Last night...no, yesterday, was wonderful, and now it was goodbye. She didn't expect him to want to stay but to leave before sunrise. If he didn't, her neighbors would see him.

Oh, if Dave had been bad, Tom's rejection would be devastating. The town would swing between calling her a hussy or patting her on the shoulder, their faces contorted in gleeful pity.

"Tom, the sun's about to rise, and so should you." She nudged him.

Her breath caught when he tightened his hold and nuzzled her neck. The sensation of his nose rubbing over her pulse sent a frisson of pleasure through her. This was what she was missing out on, being held, cherished, awaking to a new day with someone who loved her.

She yanked the duvet off, fighting the burn of tears behind her eyes. Cool air slapped her nudity, and she shivered. Her thighs ached, her sex too, but she didn't regret it. He'd been amazing, attentive, and awe-inspiring. She hefted her backside across the bed. The more distance she created between him and her, the safer her heart.

Still in the throes of sleep, he threw out a hand, patting the covers as if searching for her. Holy Tolkien, he was gorgeous: all bronzed skin and sharp indents. Her breath hitched, and she spun on a heel, darting into the bathroom. Closing the door on a click ricocheted like a bullet in the cavernous emptiness of her soul, her life. This was it for her, countless nights needing love but finding meaningless lust, instead.

She bit her lip, struggling to swallow passed the lump in her throat. Right, shower then work. Illiterate children waited for her to help them. She released a long sigh, twisted the taps to run a bath, and hoped he wouldn't be in her bed, her room, her house when she opened the door. While she waited for the tub to fill, she sorted through her day's to-do list, anything to keep her mind off the looming sadness. Between her attempts at distraction, her brain fired off reminders that she was a strong woman, not needing a man for anything other than the obvious.

She slid into the steaming water with a groan. Her muscles throbbed and twinged. Tied to the pinches of agony were the reasons for her 'suffering.' The burn on her cheeks was from the steam and not due to her wanton, irresponsible behavior. All lies. One orgasm and she'd caved.

It was too late for regrets. The blame was on her.

The bathroom door opened with a sweep of cool air. She resisted the temptation to cover herself, to look upon him, or to react to his presence. He kissed her temple, a sensual smile rolling across his lips. With his mussed hair and lustful expression, he was temptation personified. She tightened her fingers on the bath's edges.

He ran a fingertip along her nose to the tip. "Are you free for lunch?"

When her heart leaped with a 'yes,' she frowned. Normal things with him would lead to losing her heart—something she refused to do. She gripped the metaphorical band-aid on her heart, and ripped. "Why?" She pinched her lips against the wave of burning agony cinching her chest.

He jerked back, and she dipped her chin, not wanting to see the darkening of his hazel eyes. Pain had lanced across his face, and he'd tightened his jaw.

She sucked in a deep breath before taking the plunge. "Just sex, like you wanted. You don't live here, can't possibly see this going anywhere, or do you plan to uproot your big-city-life and move to Gainsford?"

She splashed water onto her face, unable to bear the emotions crossing his handsome face. Why was he upset, or was he offended? She sat up, needing to finish bathing.

Lathering the soap, she arched a brow at him standing with her sheet clasped in front of him. Couldn't he just leave like all one-night stands? She frowned.

"Sorry, was I supposed to play the weak woman and beg you to stay, to call me?" She closed her eyes against her stupidity. Men could be sensitive about things. "Tom, are you free for lunch today? How about tomorrow?"

"Fuck, Amelia, that's not what—" He pinched his lips and stomped out of the bathroom, flashing her a glimpse of his naked backside.

She heard nothing for a few minutes, then the sliding of her patio door. Only when she was certain he'd left did she allow the tears to fall. They rained amid gut-wrenching sobs. She wrapped her arms around her waist, as if they could prevent the spasms of agony from piercing her. Oh, what a fool she was. When her sobs dwindled into sniffles and the pain dulled to a constant throb, she finished bathing in the lukewarm water.

Later, the button snapped in half on her favorite dress—a pink floral fit-and-flare with puffed sleeves, a white belt, and two petticoats. The buttons were vintage, which meant a mad search for a dozen in pristine condition. She'd needed the cheerfulness of the outfit and now had to settle for something less positive.

By the time she left for work, she was running late. She hadn't eaten breakfast, having wasted time sipping coffee, lost in her thoughts as flocks of birds crisscrossed the azure sky. The various expressions on Tom's face, some she'd recognized, plagued her, as she tried to understand what his agenda was if not sex.

She moaned, expecting Liz to call for the dirty details. Amy didn't want to share, not yet. Huffing as she toddled into the library, she dumped her handbag and mobile phone onto the scarred check-out counter.

Sonja chewed on her apple with a puzzled expression on her pretty face. "Don't you have a meeting with a book vendor this morning?"

Amy squeaked, frozen in mid-step. "What?" With a cry of dismay, she snatched up her bag and phone and teetered out of the library on her black platform heels. She did have a meeting but not with the book vendor but her publisher. How could she have forgotten?

She placed her bag and phone on the trunk, using the fender for balance to shake out a pebble in her shoe. Maybe she should go home and crawl into bed? She dismissed the idea the moment it formed. Her linen still reeked of delicious, decadent sex and Tom's cologne.

Pulling off, she pressed hard on the accelerator, not wanting to be too late. Once parked haphazardly, she snatched up her bag and hurried inside Mindy's. Her stomach gurgled, reminding her of the abuse it had endured since the 'picnic.' Spotting Claire, Amy slid into the booth, a sigh escaping her.

"Whoa, bad Monday?" Claire grinned, offering a paper napkin that Amy used to dab at her beaded forehead. Sitting there in her crisp pantsuit, Claire looked out of place in small-town Gainsford. Her streaked-with-gray, brown hair belied the youthfulness of her skin.

"Not a smooth start to the week." Amy waved at Mindy for the usual order.

"So, how are things?" Claire poured sugar into her tea and stirred in clockwise circles for longer than necessary, her gaze on Amy.

"I'm working on a new series about plump women finding their matches." She bit the inside of her cheek. Unlike for her, where happily-ever-after was a fantasy and something set aside for her characters only.

"Interesting." Claire pursed her lips, placed her spoon on the saucer, and cupped her teacup in her hands. She rested her elbows on the table and sipped, a calculating expression narrowing her blue eyes. "As your...book vendor, I have to say the market's glutted at the moment."

Amy allowed a slow smile to form. "Where the main female characters are romance authors?"

Claire paused mid-sip, both eyebrows almost touching her dark-brown hairline. "Go on."

"Her name's Finley, and I'll send you what I've written so far."

Claire put her cup down with a clatter. "Good. How far are you on the next book in the Masculine Manipulation series?"

"I had something in mind, but I think it's better under my new series." Amy didn't want to say anymore, not wanting to bring Tom into the discussion, but Claire's posture said she'd wait until hell froze over. Expelling a long sigh, Amy outlined her idea about a librarian falling for a big-city banker. It took all her strength to not wince as she listed the all-too-familiar plot points.

"All right. What are you calling this series?" Claire nibbled on a cookie when Mindy slid Eggs Benedict in front of Amy.

"Thanks." Amy added sugar to her coffee while she waited for Mindy to leave. As soon as they were alone, she leaned in, almost dipping her breasts onto her plate. "Voluptuous

Virtuoso? Plump Playwrights?" She flicked a dismissive hand, spilling salt across the table. "Never mind, I'll give it more thought."

"I'll do the same." Claire pulled out her phone. "Let's diarize the next appointment before we delve into rankings and sales."

Amy nodded, bit off the corner on her toast point, then dropped it onto her plate to dig in her bag. Each second passing without finding her phone burned tension in her shoulders and hurried her search.

"Physics 530." She slumped on her bench, picturing where she'd last seen her phone—on the trunk of her car before she'd driven here in a mad dash. "I've lost my phone." She'd have to retrace her route and perhaps find it on a sidewalk.

Dread filled her chest like a wet blanket, sucking the enjoyment out of the moment. The toast tasted like sawdust, and the coffee's bitterness scalded her tongue. She hadn't backed up her contact list. Dammit.

She pushed her plate away, accepting that Monday was a wreck. "Let's not discuss sales this morning. My lost phone has me in a state."

"I can see that." Claire reached across the table to pat Amy's forearm. "I'll mail you all the details." She gathered her bag and left, a hint of her rose perfume lingering. An hour's journey north to the city of Ordmont awaited her publisher.

Amy slumped in the booth, unshed tears stinging her nostrils. She'd have liked to blame Tom for her scatter-brained day, but that wasn't fair on him. He'd done nothing but make sweet memories for her, and she'd chased him out of her life as if he was a marauder. No, she couldn't feel guilty about it. He'd have done it over lunch. She just beat him to it.

"Amy, Sonja called. Said she has your phone." Mindy chewed on her gum as she removed the plates. She slid the bill on the table and scurried off.

If only Mindy had said something before Claire left, then more guilt wouldn't tighten Amy's stomach. Her poor publisher had wasted more than two hours of her day to see her, which happened once every two months.

Slapping down notes to cover the meal, Amy hurried out to her car but drove to the library at a slower speed. The sunlight bathed her in delicious warmth, the wind cooled her heated cheeks, and the air was sweet. She strolled into the library, this time wearing a grin. Sonja finding her phone meant her day had improved, and the ominous cloud dampening her emotions could take the first bus out of Gainsford.

"Where was it?" Amy scanned the counter, searching for her digital appendage.

Sonia grimaced. "Ms. Wiggins found it on the street. She couldn't pick up the pieces on account of her rheumatism. Um, if it wasn't for the sticker on the back, I wouldn't have recognized it."

"What?" Amy squeaked, her vision spinning as her cheeks flushed cold. She grabbed the nearby bookshelf, digging her fingernails into the wood.

Sonja pulled out a clipboard, and on it, lay the remnants of a device, the little sticker Kimmy had put on it still intact. Amy cried out then cupped her mouth, trying to smother the sob. Tears streamed down her cheeks when she stretched out her hand to nudge the biggest piece with a fingertip.

"I called Mobile Den, and they said a replacement would take two to three days."

Amy nodded, forcing a smile across her stiff lips. "Thank you, Sonja."

"And this." She thumped a thick envelope on the counter. "Maude's grandson dropped it off. It's his promised pledge from yesterday's kissing booth."

Shivers racked her body, and she slumped against the bookshelf, her stomach wrenching nausea. Darkness coated her soul, and she couldn't hold back the feeling the money paid for her nocturnal services. It was a silly thought, not based on fact, but she couldn't silence it and its corresponding sadness.

Sucking in a deep breath, she tamped down her volatile emotions, aware of Sonja's furrowed brow and narrowed eyes.

"I'm taking a day off." Amy's strangled voice revealed her turmoil, and she pinched her lips before scurrying out of the library without another word.

Slamming her car door, she sat in the parking lot in a daze. The serene sunlight from earlier burned her exposed skin and the crown of her head as if it mocked her.

The wind stung her cheeks on the drive home, and the leather of the steering wheel cut into her palms, but nothing sank her spirits more than when she closed her front door. On a normal day, the coolness and silence of her home were a balm to her soul. Not today, it resonated with loneliness. There was no one to cheer her up, no one to console her.

Amid wrenching sobs, she stripped her bed, opened the windows, and settled in front of her laptop with the bottle of sherry.

Fuck the glass.

Chapter Fifteen

Tom lunged for the stack of messages his secretary, Nina, dropped onto his desk. He called himself all kinds of a fool, but his self-recrimination didn't stop him from flicking through the square blue sheets, searching for Amelia's name.

Eight days had passed, blurring time with his life falling into a dull routine. Memories and wet dreams tormented his nights. Worse, his indecisiveness added to his high levels of stress.

"She should have your mobile number. Why would she call here?" Nina arched a brow, running a judgmental gaze over him.

His shoulders slumped, and he dropped into his chair. Groaning, he leaned back to stare at the ceiling. He'd texted, phoned, and sent photos with no response. Running his palms along the arms of his chair, his thoughts spun. Short of driving there and confronting her, he didn't know how to handle this.

"Maybe she's just not that into you," Nina said, a slow smile curling her lips.

As the recipient of many a frantic woman asking for him, he'd allow her this moment. For once, a woman wasn't harassing him, but he wished she did. How the tables had turned.

"She cried after she chased me out, Nina." He closed his eyes as a fresh wave of pain swept through him, squeezing his chest as if someone crushed his heart. Her crying hadn't been the timid tears some women used to manipulate. Amelia's sobs had been gut-wrenching, heart-rending, and indicative of her emotions.

She cared for him. Then why had she pushed him away? He'd asked himself that question too many times to count.

"Fuck." He dismissed Nina and sat up to flip through the file centerstage on his desk.

Amelia Perkins aka Gemma James, was a successful author, best-seller, and recluse. Her novels ranged from sweet to hot, and he knew because he owned them all. He had to wear tight boxers to hide his permanent hard-on.

Last night, he'd haunted his usual bar. None of the women flashing come-hither looks sparked a response in him, and they should have. Most of them he'd sampled before, and to alleviate his agony, he'd thought any woman would do.

Grunting, he pulled out his phone to call Belinda—his go-to for a non-emotional quickie. She didn't answer but responded shortly afterward with a text. Decision made. Doing her tonight might help him move on from Amelia.

He liked his life in Anham, his career was on an upward trajectory, and his friends were here. Moving to Gainsford made no sense. Lust addled his mind and blurred his conviction. Time would clear his thoughts and reveal his obsession with Amelia was nothing more than pheromones.

Bounding up, he strode past Nina, shoving his phone in his pocket. "I'm heading to the gym. Take the afternoon off, and I'll see you in the morning."

"But..." Nina pursed her lips, flicked through his appointment book, then nodded.

He yanked his buzzing phone out of his pocket, checked the caller ID before pressing the phone to his ear. "Hi."

"Sorry, got my times mixed up." Belinda's sultry voice penetrated his ears, and he grinned. "Can we do earlier?"

"I'm on my way to the gym." He grimaced. Sex or gym? He needed both. "Meet you at my place?"

"Heading there now." She hung up just as the elevator door chimed.

After a swift trip to the basement and a jog to his car, he was en route to a new beginning. For once, traffic wasn't crushing, and under twenty minutes, he slid into his spot in the underground parking of his high-rise apartment. Waving to the desk guard, he took the stairs to the fifteenth floor instead of the gym, hoping to shower before Belinda arrived.

He'd just shampooed his hair when the door chimed. Cursing, he rinsed and stepped out, wrapping a towel around his dripping wet body. He pressed the buzzer to let her in, then grabbed a hand towel to rub his hair dry. Staring at himself in the bathroom mirror, he studied the dark shadows under his eyes, as if something haunted him.

More like someone: curvaceous, sensual, and addictive Amelia.

His rumpled bed and her books buried in the covers or stacked on his nightstand reflected in the mirror. He hurried to gather them, shoving them into his cupboard before pulling his linen straight.

"Tom?" Belinda called from his foyer.

"In here, sweetheart." He fluffed his pillows then scanned his room one last time.

"Oh, straight for the kill?" She laughed, her heels tapping on the marble floors.

"I need you, that's true." He smiled, leaning on the door frame to watch her stride toward him.

In a tight gray pencil skirt and a burgundy blouse, she oozed sex appeal. As a litigator, her career was her life. She had high hopes of pursuing a judgeship. Her hair gleamed like polished ebony and set her darker skin glowing. He couldn't recall how many times he'd kissed those lips.

"Your call was a surprise." She paused in front of him, trailing a finger from nipple to belly button. "It's been a while."

"Do you want coffee and a chat, or shall we get down to business?" He dropped his hand towel and gripped her waist, tugging her closer. Her spicy perfume assaulted his senses, burning his nostrils, and he fought the urge to step back. No. He locked his knees. This was Belinda with her French perfume.

"Mm, tough choice." She placed her manicured hands on his chest, her touch hot after his shower. A sensual smile curled her plump lips, and he dipped to brush his mouth across hers. Flashes of pale skin and ruby lips bombarded him, but he pushed through, sliding his tongue into Belinda's moist mouth.

No cherry met him, no tart sherry with an underlining deep addictive feminine musk.

Tightening his hold, he deepened the kiss. He could do this.

Belinda tugged his towel off and stroked her nails along the length of him. He groaned, crushing her to him as he nibbled her ear.

"Good, you're ready. I only have twenty minutes." After fisting his cock and pumping it twice, she pulled out of his arms to unbutton her blouse, exposing her white lace bra, bright against her skin. "How do you want it today?"

He unzipped her skirt, slipping a fingertip in to caress her soft skin. "On your knees, Amelia."

Belinda stiffened and arched a brow. "You didn't just call me by another woman's name, did you?"

He forced a chuckle. "Slip of the tongue?" Now why had he ended on a question?

She studied him, then buttoned her shirt closed.

No, no, no! He needed this... Her. He needed a spectacular orgasm, nothing like the last week of dismal hand jobs.

The zip sliding up ended his hopes for the night.

"I hate to say this since it will cost me a fuck-buddy, but phone her, Tom. I know our sessions are impersonal, but still, calling me 'Amelia' is insulting."

"What?" His heartbeat paused, then burst into a run. He blinked at her. "An honest mistake, Belle. It doesn't mean I care for..." But Belle swiveled on her heel and sauntered out, the front door slamming shut behind her. "Fuck."

Maybe he needed professional help? Someone who'd strip his attraction to Amelia down to the barest bones. And he couldn't blame her for his mental state, could he?

He sat on the edge of the bed, his quivering cock in hand. A slow stroke, a hard pump sent a bolt of shivers from his balls to the tip.

The memory of her bathing flashed, the soap sliding down the delicate arch of her back. Her auburn hair piled high, and the sensual curve of her breast. His orgasm took him by surprise, and he roared. For a second, he was unable to breathe through the sweet release. He pulled out and collapsed onto the bed, his legs shaking. Belinda dressing barely drew his notice. He struggled to understand what was going on.

He fell back onto his bed, staring at his ceiling in a daze. Shadows shifted across his room, measuring the passing of time, yet he didn't move. He needed to wash again. Grunting, he pulled himself up.

After his shower, he stripped his sheets, started a load of laundry, and remade his bed before collapsing on it. In the middle of a takeout call, his phone buzzed with Gram's caller ID. He froze mid-sentence, thoughts of Amelia in danger, hurt, hospitalized speared him, and he hurriedly placed his order then hung up. He called Gram back.

"Gram? Are you okay? Is Amelia...?" His chest cinched. What could he do if she was injured? She'd made it clear, sex and done. Then why the tears? And why did he care?

Gram didn't answer his questions. "Dumbass, I told you not to mess this up." She shuffled and sighed as if she tried to find a comfortable position. "Now the town thinks you dumped the girl. She's getting a ton of sympathy."

He winced, remembering how much Amelia hated their attention. Wait, he hadn't left her. "She dumped me," he roared, sitting up. "Sorry."

"Do I need to call you a dumbass again?" Her tone implied it would be better for him if she didn't. He rubbed his ear, the one she usually abused with a good boxing. "Do you like her or not?"

"It's not a question of like, Gram." Like? Mm, it was more than that, whatever this intense feeling in his chest meant.

"Being a lawyer doesn't make you smart." She sighed. "I raised you better than this."

He couldn't help but smile. "How is my upbringing tied to Amelia?"

"It's a matter of distinguishing real gold from fool's gold, my dear boy." She tutted. "So when are you visiting me? Avoiding Gainsford now that she dumped you?"

"It was a mutual decision. She didn't...dump me." He'd just said she did. Argh. "Never mind. How about this Sunday if that suits you?"

Gram hesitated. "Bring flowers."

He chuckled. "Done, and Gemma James's latest?"

"Oh, now you're talking. Love you." She hung up.

He slumped, too exhausted for words. His door chimed again, and he accepted the carton from the delivery boy. Not that he was hungry. Food had lost its appeal, and he'd had such hope when he'd placed the order. After stacking the carton in the fridge, he popped two sleeping pills he kept for emergencies. He awoke groggy but rested. No dreams had plagued him, and he dressed with a small smile. Doing Belinda had been the best idea. He'd face this day a little more himself.

When Gram called again, he was in the middle of a meeting. "Sorry, Cal, Seb, it's Gram. It might be an emergency." He flashed a smile at Cal, who waved him on. Sebastian sighed but nodded. Of the three of him, he was the cold-hearted bastard, but they loved him anyway.

"Gram?" Tom rose to stare out the glass panels at the city skyline, gray against the blue sky.

"Tom?"

Ice warred with fire to shoot down his spine. He hardened in an instant and quit breathing. Fuck. Amelia. Her voice rasped across his senses, and he almost dropped the phone.

"Amelia." Hurrying to clear his throat, he forced his thoughts to focus. "Why do you have Gram's phone?"

"She collapsed outside the library, and I don't have your number."

Fury fused a new path, and he squeezed his phone until it creaked under the abuse. "Then you shouldn't have deleted it."

"I didn't del... Physics 530, I don't have time for this. They're taking her to Gainsford Memorial. I suggest you get there."

He harumphed. "Right, like I would believe this."

"Why would I lie? You're such a donkey's backside." She hung up, leaving him staring at his blank screen.

Sexual tension zinged through him, as if he hadn't released it the night before. An image popped up on his phone, that of paramedics loading Gram into an ambulance.

He bolted.

Chapter Sixteen

TOM SKIDDED INTO THE hospital ward. Pain lanced across his shoulders from gripping the steering wheel for over an hour, but that didn't compare to the fear laying claim to his thoughts. His gaze snagged on Gram engulfed by the hospital bed. Midday sunlight streamed in through the windows, bathing her sleeping form. He paused beside the bed and stroked her parchment-like cheek, too pale for his liking.

Sharp agony seized his chest at how frail and helpless she looked. He wished she'd wake up and tease or bully him. Confronted with her age and her tenuous hold on life, he blinked to clear his vision, willing the tears not to fall. She wasn't dying, and he still had time. Not much, though.

"Hi."

A flash of fire consumed his stomach, and he twisted to meet Amelia's gaze. Fuck, the sight of her ripped his breath from him. She pushed herself out of the chair, presenting him with a full view of her lush curves in a short summer dress. The blue fabric clung to parts of her as she circled the bed.

"I booked a room for you at the bed and breakfast." She chewed on her bottom lip, and he wished he could do that for her. "I'm glad you made it. She scared me when she fainted." Her fingers twitched as if she longed to touch him, or his presence made her uncomfortable. "I'm so sorry, Tom."

She raised her hand to squeeze his, but he grabbed it and tugged her into his arms. A moan escaped when her exotic fragrance surrounded him. He sucked in a deep breath and let it out in a shudder. Her curves molded to him, and her rubbing his back did more than soothe him. His cock pulsed a greeting.

Sighing, he buried his face in the curve of her neck, wishing he could press a kiss there. He had no right. She didn't want him. Ice drenched him, and he forced his arms to release her.

"Thank you, Amelia."

She nodded and strolled out of the ward. He stared at the door long after she'd left his line of sight. Everything within him demanded he rush after her, and he had to grit his teeth to stop himself from calling to her.

"Dumbass," Gram muttered.

"Gram." He smiled, fluffing her pillow. "How are you feeling? What did the doctor say?"

"Low blood pressure. He's drawn so much blood I feel like a deflated balloon." A splash of pink flushed Gram's cheeks, and she looked almost herself. "He might as well check whether I have Viking in my genetics."

He snorted. "You gave me quite a scare." Perhaps it would be wise to set up an office here in Gainsford. To be closer to Gram, no other reason. He didn't need to be in court full time, and he could work on other cases. Sighing, he curled his fingers around her hand, trying not to bruise her.

She tutted. "I fainted. Could've been the heat or an inner-ear infection. I'm fine, I promise, Tom." She squeezed his hand and offered a timid smile. It couldn't counter the dark circles under her eyes.

"Need anything?"

She shook her head. "Amy's fetching a few things for me."

"Amelia is..." He frowned, not liking that Gram had to rely on a...stranger?

"She's a sweet girl, my boy." Gram gestured to her pedestal. "She left my phone. I'll call you when the doctor has the results." Gram smothered a yawn. "Chocolate, flowers, Gemma James, bring those at visiting hour."

He chuckled. "What? No diamonds? Wine?"

"No one likes a smartass." She grinned, love for him pouring from her gaze. "Except your gram."

"Love you too." He tucked her in, kissed her temple, and left. First, he'd need to buy a few clothing items. He'd driven straight from the office. Then he needed to talk to Amelia.

Fuck. And say what? How much he obsessed about her? That one night hadn't been enough for him? Or…use the town to get what he wanted? Mm.

"Cal," Tom said into his phone the moment Callum answered. "We need to talk."

"How's Gram?"

"Don't know yet. We're waiting for the bloodwork. She doesn't have many years left in her." Tom grimaced, pushing those dismal thoughts to the back of his mind. "I might have to set up a satellite office here."

"It's doable. If you still come in for meetings or attend court when needed." His voice muffled as if he put his hand across his phone. "Seb says he has a few cases for you. He'll take over whatever you're still working on."

"He will?" Tom arched a brow. He'd always thought Seb barely tolerated him.

"Yup. Neglecting your only living relative is stupid. His words."

"I…I don't know what to say." Tears threatened to fall again. "I'm touched, Cal. Tell Seb he has my gratitude."

"Finding Chrissie changed my perspective, and Seb's got his baby sister to think of. We got you, Tom."

The next call was to Nina. After explaining the situation and that her job wasn't in jeopardy, he gave her a list of instructions. If anyone could help him, it was his no-nonsense legal secretary.

With his new clothes in the trunk of his car, he waited outside the library. Many library members threw strange glances at him, some with anger, others with pity. He sighed. Amelia had to deal with this censure? The sun had started to set when she locked the front door and halted, her gaze resting on him.

She drew in a deep breath that jiggled her breasts, squared her shoulders, and crossed the empty street. "How's she doing?" She lowered her bag, catching the straps with her fingers before sliding it the last bit to the ground. "Maude was fine when I dropped off her things. The hospital didn't call…"

"I've missed you." He winced. Not what he should have started with but true, nonetheless.

Amelia gasped, and goosebumps broke out on her bare forearms when she shivered.

"Why did you chase me out? Why didn't you call?" His voice roughened with the amount of emotion churning in his gut. He wanted to touch her, hold her, and kiss those sweet lips. "Why didn't you respond to my missed calls, texts, voice messages?"

"I…" She pinched her lips, shaking her head, and tears shimmered in her eyes.

The sight of them twisted a metaphorical dagger in his chest, and he pressed his hand over his heart as if his touch could ease the ache deep within.

His gaze lingered on her braided auburn hair, wishing he could unravel it. He settled for tucking a curl behind her ear. "I heard you crying."

She stumbled back, her eyes wide and her face paler. "You…did?"

"Why chase me out, Amelia?"

She tightened her grip on her bag and averted her gaze. "The sun was rising."

"Out of your life, not home." He shortened the distance between them. "You ended us before we began."

"Us?" She snorted, leveling her brown gaze on him. "You wanted me in your bed, Tom. Why should I let you have more than that?"

"Because I want more."

Her laughter lacked warmth. "Right."

"So stubborn," he growled, stiffening his arms to stop himself from throwing his hands into the air or grabbing hers. "I want more of you, of this. I want us."

"Fine, visit me on weekends, well, maybe only Saturdays, because, y'know, work needs your Fridays, and you have to be back by Sunday night. I can see this working out perfectly."

He frowned. "That's not what I was—"

"I *told* you I don't do one-night-stand jockeys." She huffed and spun on her navy-blue heels.

"You did this jockey, and you'll damn well do me again." He looped an arm around her shoulders and tilted her back. She squealed, but she was at his mercy. If she struggled, he could drop her. "Are you scared I'll break your heart? Of what the townsfolk will say?"

Her grip on his biceps tightened when he slid a hand farther up her back. "This is insane…and unrealistic."

"So both then? Did you once consider you might be breaking my heart? Is this all about you, Amelia?"

She stilled, her gaze meeting his. Her lips parted as if she wanted to disparage him, but her walnut-colored eyes warmed.

"I've read your books, Ms. James, that's how serious I am."

She squeaked. "What?" Color drained then flushed her cheeks. "You know?" Fear darkened her eyes, and he hated seeing it.

"Fuck, Amelia, do you think I'd tell anyone?" He whipped her up, creating distance between them when she was steady on her heels. "You don't know me at all."

She nodded, running her palms down the skirt of her dress. "I don't."

Well, that was a start. "My favorite color is green."

Her peach lips parted before she clamped them shut.

"I have eclectic tastes in music. I don't understand art but love sculptures that capture movement. I don't like sushi."

"No sushi?" A smile teased her lips. "That's a deal-breaker, Tom."

He sidled closer, gripping her hips to angle her body. "I like you in your delicate sleepwear, in your leggings, in these dresses, or wearing nothing at all." He nuzzled her neck above her pulse. She shivered again. "You're not ticklish on your toes, you have a kind heart, and you care about the community."

She harumphed but didn't pull out of his arms. It gave him hope, so he tested his boundaries, tugging her deeper into his embrace.

"As charming as you are, Mr. Bradshaw, it's just sex between us."

He released a shuddering breath. "I won't lie. It's taking all my control not to kiss you."

Her breath caught, and her fingertips dug into his muscles. She trembled, yet she pulled out of his arms. "I rest my case."

Clutching her bag to her chest, she sidled back, creating more distance between them than he liked.

While running a hand over his face, he sighed. He wasn't winning today. "Can I walk you home?"

She shook her head, scanned the street both ways before crossing it. Her mumbled 'good night' barely reached his ears.

He watched her hurry down the street, not once glancing over her shoulder. The second between sunset and the streetlamps flickering on reflected his soul and the darkness nestled there. Pain seeped into every pore, as if the light that made his life worthwhile had faded, and only loneliness loomed. He spun on his heel and paused. Across the street, opposite the library was a house for sale. The potential lay in the ranch-style architecture with a wraparound porch, a minimal yard, and an overgrown pathway to a red front door.

Climbing into his car, he texted Nina, then tossed his phone on the passenger seat before starting the engine. He had tonight to strategize because tomorrow, he would set his plan into motion; to woo Amelia. Seeing her had solidified her place in his life, and her reticence was but a stumbling block.

With one last glance at the house, he pulled out of the parking spot. A small smile played across his lips, reflected in the rearview mirror. He would call in the big guns: Dave and Liz.

Chapter Seventeen

AMY PINCHED HER NOSE, fighting the burn of exhaustion. She squeezed her eyes shut against the grit and cursed Tom under her breath. He'd thought she'd tossed his number in a fit of pique. Oh, Holy Tolkien. And he'd heard her crying like a toddler who'd lost her toy.

Heat flared across her cheeks, and she sighed, dropping her hand. What did it matter? Maude would recover, and he'd return to Anham. Amy only had to resist him for a day or two. Easier said than done. Last night, his warmth and intoxicating cologne had poured off his body. Memories of their time together lashed across her control, tearing at the foundation of her willpower.

His pain had been the final catalyst. He'd looked and sounded as if she'd hurt him, broken his heart. She huffed and grabbed a stack of books, needing to keep herself busy.

"I heard a certain someone is in town." Sonja didn't look up from the magazine she thumbed through. "Mindy has it, he has his eye set on you."

Amy snorted. So he'd said, and she'd countered him with logic. He'd be a fool to pursue her. "He can set both eyes on me, he's still a slick city banker passing through."

"And what if he stays?" Sonja peered over the top of the magazine.

"For how long?" Amy shook her head. "He'll grow bored, resentful." She flashed a smile she was far from feeling. "Us small-town girls can't compete with the sophistication of city women."

Sonja chuckled. "I bet you could handle him, Amy. You've got loads of class and attitude."

This time, Amy's smile was swift as warmth flooded her chest. "Thanks, Sonja. Still, he's after one thing, and I don't want to go through the town's ridicule over events real and fictional." She sorted the books on the returns trolley. "Already with him in town, folks are speculating. He only has to look at me, and off they go on some tangent. Their comments will swing to whore or spinster with nothing between."

"Don't let their opinions doom you to a lonely life, Amy."

"Easy for you to say, Sonja. As high school sweethearts, you didn't have the town as your chaperones."

Sonja shrugged, closed the magazine, and slipped it onto the rack. "So date him in private."

"Nothing stays hidden." Amy paused, staring at the woman who strode into the library. A crisp gray pant suit clung to a lithe figure. Her black hair was pinned up with no strands escaping. She had a classical beauty, almost timeless, and an air of frigidity.

"Hi." Sonja smiled.

The woman nodded but settled her dark gaze on Amy. "I see," she said. "I'm Nina." She flicked her fingers behind her. "My boss just bought the house across from the library. I need to make it move-in ready. I wanted to apologize for the traffic coming through and the use of the parking area."

"Oh, this is wonderful." Amy beamed. "Welcome to Gainsford."

Nina shook her head. "I'm not staying for long. There are a few repairs needed, fresh paint, and signage. I might visit, though. Gainsford seems like an oasis of tranquility and friendliness." She smiled, but it looked strained as if smiling was rare for her. "Its authenticity is refreshing."

"I hope you enjoy your stay. I'm Amy, and this is Sonja. Let us know if there's anything we can help with."

"That's so kind of you." Nina ran another appraising gaze over Amy before nodding and sauntering out.

"Weird," Sonja said. "She liked the look of you, though." She giggled. "I didn't exist. Mm, seems like your love life is looking up."

Amy snorted. "Woman or man, it matters not. I'll be the talk of the town, again."

"The Dave incident was years ago. I'm sure they've forgotten all about that." Sonja thumped a box of old books onto the counter. "Want to take this to the back for me?"

Amy sighed then arched a brow. "For a coffee?"

"Deal." Sonja skipped across to the door leading to the kitchenette.

Amy grabbed the box and staggered under its weight. Whispers, a giggle reached her as she stashed it in the pristine storeroom. When she returned to the desk, there was a massive bouquet of red roses. Sonja buried her face in the opening buds.

"Wow. Is it your wedding anniversary?" As Amy inched closer, the fragrance of the flowers tickled her nose. It twitched as she fought off a sneeze. No, not now. Fear gripped her, and she leaped back on another sneeze.

"Nope. These are for you." Sonja beamed, holding a card out to her.

"Me?" Amy gasped. Never had she received such a bouquet. Each rose was perfect, as if chosen with care. Not a single petal wilted. She took the card, her hand trembling.

Tom had scrawled one word. *To us.*

Her heart fluttered when her world tilted. She gripped the counter as her face flushed cold. How could she fight him if he did sweet things like this?

"It's from him, isn't it?"

Amy sneezed twice before stumbling away from the bouquet. "It's yours if you take it home now."

"Dang, Amy, I forgot about your allergy." Sonja ran around the library, opening windows before sweeping the roses outside.

Tears streamed down Amy's cheeks. Her eyes itched and burned. She dug in her bag for her medication, swallowing one with a scalding sip of coffee. "He's trying to kill me," she wheezed. In his defense, he hadn't known, and she hadn't volunteered the information. *My favorite color is green.*

"Um, Amy..." Sonja had returned empty-handed and now read the medication bottle. "These expired last year."

"What?" Amy wiped her eyes, trying to read the label through her tears. She sneezed and blew her running nose with a tissue as she squinted at the bottle in disbelief. "I'm just going to—"

She swayed, sneezed again, and scratched her neck, wincing when her nails scraped across her sensitive skin.

"Your face is swelling." Sonja gripped her by the elbow and ushered her to her small Ford. "I'll drive."

The cloying sweetness of the roses engulfed her from the trunk of the car. Amy moaned, pins and needles merged with itchiness, and when she scratched, a fresh wave of pain pulsed. She curled into a ball on the backseat of Sonja's car. Between sneezes, scratches, and coughs, she lost track of time. When the side door opened, and cool air rushed in, she sighed then shivered.

"Allergic reaction to roses," Sonja told the nurses.

They lifted Amy onto a gurney and wheeled her into the ER where a doctor waited to assess her. Pain warred with self-pity, and she sobbed, wishing someone would knock her out. She cursed herself and Tom too many times to count. If she'd followed his lead, he'd have known not to send her flowers. Some artificial scents affected her, which is why she imported her oils. They were the only ones that didn't make her sick.

Injections and ointment followed. She snuggled in the bed until the itching had subsided, and she could see through her swollen eyes. When she couldn't sleep another minute, she climbed off the bed.

Since she was in the hospital, she might as well check in with Maude. It didn't take long to reach her ward. "How are you feeling, Maude?" Amy lowered her aching body into the chair she'd occupied yesterday. She took the time to tuck in her hospital gown, not needing to flash the poor woman.

"Amelia? What happened? Why are you so...splotchy?"

"Your dear grandson sent me flowers." Amy grimaced. "It was a sweet gesture."

"He's such a dumbass." Maude huffed, pulling herself into a sitting position but sinking into the pillows canceled her efforts.

"Agreed, but to be fair, he didn't know." Amy closed her eyes against her looming future. "It's a matter of time before the town hears of this." Tears burned behind her eyes as if she hadn't cried out a year's supply in the last few hours. "I'll be a laughing stock."

"Bored people need something to entertain them, Amy. No matter what you do, you can't avoid them. As the censure wheel spins, everyone gets a turn."

"I've had my turn." She whimpered, pinching her lips against any other escaping sounds.

Silence fell, and she watched the dust motes dancing in the sunlight streaming in through the windows. Maude sipped her tea, her movements sure, belying her recent fainting spell.

Her cup clinked onto the metallic tray. "Do you care for Tom?"

Amy gasped, then dropped her chin to her collarbone. Revealing what he invoked in her wouldn't help the situation, but under Maude's vigilant gaze, she couldn't lie. She nodded. "Stupid me."

"To fall in love is never stupid."

Amy snorted. "It is when he's a philanderer."

Maude grinned. "Falling for the consummate rake? How cliché."

Amy chuckled despite the pain cinching her chest as if Cupid had reached through her rib cage and used her heart like a stress ball. "I see the similarities."

"Yet the premise still stands. Rakes make the best husbands."

All the historical romance novels Maude must have read in her lifetime was the source of her confidence. Amy grinned. "Hell, I'd settle for a man who lives nearby. Long-distance relationships never work out."

"True, he can't woo you unless he's here." Maude tapped her chin. A calculating expression crossed her delicate features.

That didn't bode well. Amy threw out her hands in a subconscious plea. "I'm not saying I'd date your grandson if he lived in Gainsford." If Tom stayed, she wouldn't stand a chance. He'd drown her convictions with his steely determination. "And don't you dare tell him how I feel about him."

Maude grinned. "Our secret. Let him work for what he wants."

Amy sighed. That wasn't what she'd meant at all.

"Here you are." Sonja skipped into the ward wearing a bright smile. "You look much better." She waved a paper bag. "I have your meds, and the doctor's discharged you. I called Liz."

Dave entered as if on cue. Concern darkened his eyes. He strode across the room and swept Amy into a crushing hug. "Good, you're fine. Liz is in a panic. I rushed ahead to warn you."

With her face shoved in his shirt, she couldn't free herself. Tears threatened again, and she grumbled about the pitfalls of being a woman. When he released her, he nodded at Maude and Sonja.

"Gave us quite a scare." His fingers lingered on her elbow as if Amy might faint where she stood.

"Your dating life is going to kill me." Liz hurried in to wind Amy in a suffocating hug.

"It's just an allergic reaction." She shrugged like she hadn't wanted to die an hour ago.

Dave pulled out his phone and stormed from the room. Amy gaped at his exit, his unusual rudeness startling.

"Scared Dave too. He's never had a sister, and since your truce, he's embraced you as his family." Liz ushered Amy into the chair, and Sonja handed over the meds before leaving, mentioning her plans to air out her car and the library.

"I'm better, in fact, the doctor's discharged me." Amy waved her paper bag. "I want a long bath." She rose to her feet, forcing Liz to shift. "Maude, let me know if you need anything."

"I'm going home too, and thank you, Amy."

She squeezed the older woman's hand and returned to her ward, trailing a stomping Liz.

"Just like that? You could've gone into anaphylactic shock."

Amy chuckled. "It's like poison ivy, Liz, and you know it."

"Yes, but it's been years since your last reaction." She pouted, watching Amy dress, her fingers twitching as if she wanted to help button her blouse.

"A ride home, maybe a little chicken soup, and I'll be right as rain in the morning."

"Damn Tom and his romantic ideas." Liz pinched her lips, falling beside Amy as they strolled to the car.

The trip home was in silence. Each step she took toward her front door was as if steel-lined concrete shoes weighed her down. Her bag hung on her doorknob, thanks to Sonja's thoughtfulness. Amy waved at Liz, hoping her sister wouldn't linger.

"I'll send Dave with the soup."

Amy nodded, unhooked her bag, unlocked the door, and closed it behind her along with her dreams of reformed rakes.

Chapter Eighteen

IF ONE MORE PERSON knocked on her door to offer veiled concern, Amy would give them an uncensored piece of her mind. In her leggings and a baggy T-shirt, she'd buried herself in her current novel, Finley having persuaded Duke to drop his wet clothes for shared warmth. The next scene would be a delicious one to write.

Her kink-armoire's door gaped, with whips, cuffs, collars peeking out, all serving as inspiration. Not expecting to see Tom standing at her sliding door, she squeaked, clutching her chest to appease her thumping heart.

She unlocked the door. "What?"

His dark hair flopped across his temple, and his intense gaze snagged hers. "I just heard. I'm so sorry, Amelia. I can't apologize enough."

"All's forgiven. How could you have known?" She tugged on the door as if the conversation was over when the sight of him in his low-riding jeans, thick boots, and tight T-shirt did more for her libido than staring at her closet had. Her gaze dipped again, and she forced it to settle on his face, his chin, his jaw, and those soft lips. Holy Dostoyevsky, the man was lethal.

His hand caught the door, and the look he leveled on her implied he hadn't said his piece. She huffed, stepping aside to let him in. He followed, crowding her with his spicy cologne, his chest an inch from her straining breasts drove her back. When her backside bumped against her desk, she glared at him. A slow smile curled his lips, and her stomach leaped and danced. He wrapped his long fingers around her neck, slid them down to her collarbone to rub his thumb across her exposed skin.

Then he gripped her upper arms. "How are you feeling?"

"I'm well, just irritated with all these interruptions." She yanked her arms free and rested her palms on his chest to shove him. He didn't budge; instead, he settled his hands on her hips as if he had the right to. She curled her fingers into fists, preparing to pound his chest for release.

"Now, do you see the importance of telling me about you? Any other allergies I need to know of?"

She pursed her lips. "No." Under his concern, she unfurled her fingers, splaying them out on his pecs. Beneath her touch, his heart thumped a steady beat. It called to her, and she wished she could press her ear to his chest and let him hold her.

"Good." His shoulders slumped as tension eased out of him. "I—" His head snapped up, and his focus snagged on her gaping armoire. "Fuck." He dropped his gaze to her upturned face, and his fingers flexed where they touched her.

"What's the matter?" She twisted to see what had alarmed him, but he was too close to grant her much leeway.

"You make it so damn difficult not to think of you as the woman I dream of and ache for."

She stilled at the sight of her gaping closet and his words, delivered in his rough baritone. He dreamed of her, ached? An intense throbbing in her core and lower had her squeezing her thighs tight. Her face matched the heat coiling in her belly. "It's research."

He shuddered and swept her hair off her temple before cupping her cheeks. "I didn't come here to kiss you." His voice was soft, just above a husky whisper, as if emotion overwhelmed him. "I want to, don't get me wrong."

His gaze lingered on her lips, and she tightened her fingers into his pecs. His breath puffed across her chin, and the air thickened with sexual tension and unsaid words.

"It's royal blue. My favorite color." She licked her dry lips. The quicker she shared something, the sooner he'd leave. And the way her resolve was crumbling, she needed him out of her home fast. "I like most genres of music, but Ella Fitzgerald is my go-to. I prefer Art Nouveau architecture to art, but now and then, a piece will summon a powerful reaction in me. I like you in these jeans, in your running shorts, and with nothing on." Accepting that she toyed with hellfire, she feathered her fingers from his neck, along his shoulders to his biceps. His breath hitched, and the green in his eyes swirled and stormed. "You're stubborn, determined, opinionated, and arrogant, but you adore Maude."

He grinned, and the appearance of his dimples scattered her heartbeat. "Is that my only redeeming quality?"

She blinked, gaping like a fish out of water. Her thoughts danced out of reach, and her throat seized from his smile. Holy Darwin, even after all this time, he devastated her senses.

"Amelia." He rasped her name and dipped his head to run his lips across hers.

She inhaled sharply, taking a little of his breath inside her. He pulled away, and she followed his retreating lips, then shook her head to clear it.

"Um, you're kind too." She squeezed her eyes shut against her fumbling. Why did he fluster her so? With his hard edges pinning her, his cologne dazzling her, she couldn't think. She resorted to instinct, which in his case, was potent, addictive lust.

"I want to know everything about you, Amelia. Your preferred breakfast, how you like your coffee, what's on your bucket list, who was your first kiss. Aren't you the slightest bit curious about me?"

The hope in his eyes pierced through the layers coating her heart, and she released a long sigh. "Yes."

He arched his back on a bark of laughter. "At last."

One second, she admired his joy and the way it added to his handsomeness. The next, he claimed her mouth, sliding his tongue in with a groan. He wrapped his arms around her, trapping her within his embrace. She tried to stay firm but melted, her body making demands she was helpless to deny.

He leaped back, and she stumbled at the loss of his support, but he threw out his hands to catch her. Once she was steady, he strode to the opposite side of the lounge. With his back to her, and his shoulders rising and falling with every jarring breath, she realized the kiss had affected him as much as it had her.

"We'll have our first date in seven days." He dropped his forehead into his palm. "I'm not sure how I'll survive until then, but we'll try it your way, Amelia." He stormed across to her and kissed her temple, with his lips lingering.

Then he was gone, the sliding door clicking with the same finality as when she'd chased him out.

Staring outside for the longest time, she held her fingertips to her tingling lips. She was drowning, barely keeping herself above water. Below in the depths within her, heartache waited for her, and somehow she knew, with Tom, she wouldn't recover.

And since she was in love with him already, the edges of her heart twanged, spreading despair. She could embrace this time with him, savor each moment, smile, and delicious kiss. Or she could push him away and wallow in self-pity that was her fate anyway.

Her phone rang, and she lunged for it, grateful for the disruption. "Liz."

"How are you feeling?" At her motherly tone, Amy smiled.

She couldn't say she throbbed with need, her thoughts spinning out of control and her resistance slipping. "Good."

"Dave's livid. He wants a piece of Tom for this."

Amy frowned. Dave's protectiveness felt odd. Then again, she hadn't been sick or hospitalized in the time she'd known him. He might have reacted the same before.

"It's not Tom's fault. He didn't know, and now he does."

There was a lull with Kimmy giggling in the background. "You saw him?"

"He came by to apologize." Amy brushed her fingers across her lips. And what an apology.

"Oh, well, then...that's good." Liz's awkward response drew Amy away from reliving Tom's steamy kisses.

"What's the matter?"

She huffed. "Nothing, just worried, that's all. Want to meet me for pancakes tomorrow?"

Amy grinned. "Sure." Whenever they were sick as kids, their mother would offer pancakes as an incentive to get better faster. She chuckled, like a cold wouldn't run its course regardless.

After hanging up, she ran a bath, soaked until her toes and fingers were prunes before she curled into bed. She didn't bother to pull on pajamas, instead, she lay there, one hand cupping a breast with her thumb stroking a pebbled nipple. On a soft sigh, she drifted off to the memory of Tom in her bed.

Chapter Nineteen

Tom played dirty. He was a man on a mission, and he needed allies. Cupping his coffee, he endured Dave's glare and Liz's knowing smirk with dignity, or so he hoped. After yesterday's tragedy, that they'd invited him in this early in the morning was something to be grateful for.

When Gram had told him about Amelia's allergic reaction, he'd driven to her home like a madman. The all-consuming fear, as debilitating as what Gram invoked in him, had solidified his *condition* in his mind.

He was in love.

He winced and sipped his coffee to hide it.

"Don't get me wrong, Tom, but you're messing this up." Liz glanced at Dave.

"I helped you because I thought your intentions were pure." Dave loomed, rolling his shoulders, and Tom half expected the man to slam his fist into his palm.

"I do, but she's stubborn. Has this fear I'll rip her heart out." Tom dipped his head as he recalled Amelia's upturned face, the pain in her warm brown eyes. "To set your minds at ease, I'm moving to Gainsford, even bought a house."

"Oh." Liz bounced in her chair. "And you're here to ask for our blessing?"

Tom nodded. "I need to woo her, and I thought to include the town."

"That's fighting dirty." Dave chuckled, his shoulders relaxing. "Since I've already aided your quest, count me in."

"Dave," Liz gasped, yet her lips curled into a smile that shot darts of need through Tom.

It was so reminiscent of Amelia, that he couldn't help but delve into his memories. He loved when Amelia smiled at him like that, as if he held a special place in her heart. A dull ache laced with eternal hope claimed his chest, and he rose to his feet. He needed to check in with Nina.

Liz rose too. "We're meeting for pancakes within the hour. You could be at Mindy's before we arrive?"

Warmth spread through his chest as if he'd had a shot of whisky. He grinned. "Thank you." He captured her hand for a squeeze, then pumped Dave's hand.

Excitement pulsed through him as he jogged to his car. He'd stop off at his new home, then head for Mindy's. The sale had happened fast since he'd paid cash. Now all he had to do was wait for the renovations to finish. Nina had impeccable taste. He'd issued a must-have list but left everything up to her.

It was such a short distance, and the lack of traffic was refreshing. He arrived outside the library with the grin still splitting his cheeks.

"Nina?" He shuffled inside the house opposite the library and laughed, too joyful for words.

She'd furnished his waiting room already. It had only needed a fresh coat of paint. Large leather couches lined the walls, a Persian carpet on the floor, plants, and paintings from local artists completed the décor. He peeked into his office furnished with a massive mahogany desk. Old school but perfect. His law books and articles filled the floor-to-ceiling mahogany bookshelves, and satin curtains filtered out the morning sunlight.

A new door blocked off the remainder of the house. He opened it. Here the paint and glue odors were the strongest. He trod on paper sheets protecting the wooden floorboards toward the banging echoing through the house.

"Nina?"

She popped her head into the passage. "Morning." Gliding into full view, she wore jeans and a T-shirt, with her black hair braided. He'd never seen her this casual. "When you decided to do this, I thought you had the balls to ask me, your legal secretary. Tom, I'm loving this assignment. Hell, I might consider moonlighting as an interior designer." She grinned.

"You've done an amazing job so far. How much longer before I can move in?"

"The bones of this place were in excellent condition, so it's mostly cosmetic. Oh, and I ordered a full reno on your kitchen."

Made sense. The previous kitchen had to have been a little antiquated. He frowned, counting the number of doors lining the passage. "Three bedrooms? Isn't that a bit much?"

"The price of the house was a bargain. I'm adding a sunroom to serve as your lounge and a revamp of your en suite and second bathroom. You will be able to have guests, with a spare room for a nursery."

His breath hitched when he imagined a miniature-Amelia running down the passage to leap into his arms. "Three bedrooms might not be enough. Amelia is a twin."

Nina dug in her pocket and offered him a torn piece of paper. "It's her new number." She spun on her heel, then paused. "I met her yesterday, Tom. I approve." Nina disappeared into another room before popping her head out again. "She drove over her mobile last Monday. That's why she has a new number and didn't respond to your texts or calls."

The lingering bitterness dissolved. Bright light splintered his soul, and he sighed, tossing a grateful smile at Nina. "Thank you."

Minutes later, he parked his car outside Mindy's and strode in, sliding into his usual booth. "Morning, Mindy." He beamed, accepting the menu she offered him. He'd already had breakfast, but he'd eat a ton of pancakes if it meant seeing Amelia.

"Welcome back, Tom." Mindy's weak smile revealed her opinion of him and negated her welcome. "What will you have?"

"A little advice, if you could spare it." He relaxed his shoulders, hoping to ease the tension now that he faced the second task in his strike plan. "I'm here to woo a certain librarian. She's being stubborn."

"Woo?" Mindy smiled. "So, you're staying?"

He nodded.

She laughed, drawing customers's attention. "I knew it. It's the way you look at her, dear boy."

"It is?" He could recall only once when he'd been in Mindy's. Yes, he'd wanted to devour Amelia then too.

"Don't give up, shower her with sincere compliments, and sign up for her community projects." She popped her gum. "Dave broke her heart, but he was never the one for her." She ran her gaze over him. "You can handle her."

Tom shook his head. "I'm struggling."

"Takes a strong man to admit that."

"Well, she's unique, and I blundered it in the beginning." He grimaced, remembering their failed date and her fake orgasm. Not that she counted it as a date, yet she'd dressed to impress. He shifted on his ass with the familiar ache intensifying. "And yesterday."

"So I heard. Stunning bouquet, though. Try chocolates instead."

"Thank you, Mindy. After yesterday, candy might be safer." Dipping his head, he studied the menu. "A coffee and a stack of your finest pancakes." He grinned.

"With bacon?"

"Sure."

After Mindy scurried off, he pulled the torn piece of paper out of his pocket to update Amelia's details on his phone. Then he texted her but drew in a deep breath before sending it.

Join me for coffee at Mindy's?

Mindy brought him coffee, distracting him from checking his phone for a response. Yet the ping of a text message spiked dopamine through him. His wide smile was a weak celebration of this small victory.

Morning, heading there for pancakes. A Perkins tradition.

She didn't invite him to join her, and his mini-celebration fizzled.

You can meet us there if you want.

He whooped, then flashed everyone an apologetic smile. His emotions see-sawed, like a teenager in the first flush of puppy love, but the happiness welling inside him was too addictive to overlook. He loved her, but the hows and whys, he couldn't say. From the moment he'd met her, she'd spun his thoughts, burned desire through him, and still did. And despite every new thing he learned about her, it didn't appease his curiosity, this need to be with her, to see her.

He'd awoken to her within his arms and had feigned asleep when she'd stirred because he hadn't wanted to admit, even to himself, how much he wanted to stay with her. Chasing him out had cracked his heart, and bitter anger had seeped in. If he'd stayed and fought for her, where would they have been now? Then again, he hadn't wanted to change his 'perfect' life in Anham.

The bell chimed to Liz and Dave strolling in, hand in hand. They slid into his booth, sitting opposite him. Dave waved at Mindy, gesturing with his fingers that they'd like two of what Tom was having.

"Morning. Imagine seeing you here." Liz smiled, cuddling into Dave's side since he'd thrown his arm across the backrest.

"Felt like pancakes," he said around a mouthful of sweet, buttery goodness. "Amelia said this was a Perkins tradition?" He listened as Liz explained, but his gaze kept flicking to the door, expecting Amelia to arrive and not wanting to miss it.

"So, your roses brought this on. I've been craving pancakes for ages."

"How's the baby doing?" Tom sipped his coffee, admiring the pink on Liz's cheeks. Amelia would look as beautiful pregnant with his child.

"Well." Dave patted Liz's belly before stealing a kiss.

The doorbell chimed, and Tom straightened, raising his hopeful gaze to the door. He moaned, memorizing Amelia in her three-quarter burgundy leggings and a red polka-dot white sweetheart halter top. Her hair curled over one shoulder, and burgundy lipstick accentuated her lips.

He clambered off the bench, gesturing to her to slide in. Her scent hit him first, and he pinched his lips, his nostrils flaring. Fuck. Then she brushed past him, and shivers rippled over his skin.

"Morning, how are you feeling?" Liz poured sugar into her coffee.

"Good." Amelia flashed a smile at Tom. "This is a surprise."

"I was here when I texted you. Then Liz and Dave arrived." Tom forced a shrug, but his muscles were too tense, with her warmth reaching him across the inches between them. He looped his arm around her shoulders and tugged her into the curve of his body, all to kiss her temple. "Morning, beautiful."

She blushed.

Taking pity on her, he opted for a change of subject. "I'm visiting Gram at the retirement village if you want to join me."

Amelia chewed on her bottom lip. "I'd love to come if it's not too much of an imposition."

"You're never an imposition." He dipped his head to kiss her ear. "Stop nibbling on your lip. It's driving me crazy."

She gasped and met his gaze before settling on his lips. Mindy saved him from yet another blunder, and he shifted, creating distance between their thighs. The lost warmth summoned a frown, so he laced his fingers through hers and pinned their clasped hands to his thigh. Sitting here with her and her family was progress. It wasn't enough for him, though. He wanted to kiss her, to bring joy to her face, but in her presence, he struggled to be himself, to use his usual suave comments.

He couldn't afford to push her away.

She meant too much to him.

Chapter Twenty

When Tom texted, Amy had been at the library helping Nina choose furniture and finishes. The woman was in a panic, unable to decide, and needed to impress her boss with her choices. Amy had gone with large couches, leather wingbacks, and bared brick for the lounge.

Creams and whites for the kitchen with stainless steel appliances added warmth to the room. She'd waved goodbye as she'd hurried out to Mindy's, promising to drop by in a day or two. After their initial meeting, Nina had become a familiar face, needing guidance in her first renovation. Sonja had volunteered Amy's services since she'd redone her properties the previous year.

Seeing Tom sitting there in a booth with her sister and Dave sucked the air out of Amy's lungs. She pasted on a smile, despite her stuttering heartbeat and the excitement zinging through her veins. If he stayed, this was what it could be like, meeting the man of her dreams for a coffee at Mindy's.

But he wasn't staying.

He was so stubborn, not understanding that his fake affection made it more difficult for her. She scanned the diner and glanced away to hide her shock. Sweet smiles and nods crossed the familiar faces when she met their gazes. Where was their usual censure? Their disdain? She flicked a glance at Tom to find his focus on her, with something intense swirling in his eyes.

"Did you order?" he asked.

She shook her head, not trusting her voice. Tears pressed behind her eyes, a meltdown looming. She was such a fool to love this man.

"Want the same?" He pointed to his half-eaten pancakes.

She nodded, wishing she could pull her hand free from his grasp. Clenching her jaw, she lambasted her weak heart. She was stronger than this, independent, successful, loved.

Tugging her hand out of his, she gestured to Mindy, who nodded from across the diner. Then Amy sat on her hands so he wouldn't hold one hostage again.

"What did the doctor say?" Maude was the safest topic since her sister and brother-in-law showed no inclination of participating in the conversation or to rescue her. They'd taken a backseat when just yesterday, both had wanted to lay into Tom.

Flicking her hand over, she pinched the underside of her thigh and winced. This wasn't a dream, and she couldn't remember falling through an interdimensional portal.

"Just a fainting spell. Still, at her age, it was grounds for concern." He squeezed her knee, and Amy stifled a squeak. Heat poured into her from his touch when he didn't remove his hand. "It's why I'm moving to Gainsford."

"What?" She met his gaze to find him staring at her again. He was staying?

"Anham is no longer my home. I'm keeping my apartment since there will be court dates I'll need to attend. For the majority of my time, my life will be here."

"You're a...lawyer?" A buzzing in her ears blurred his words, and she blinked at him. Heat stormed up her neck to claim her cheeks, and she fought the urge to fan herself.

"I'll set up an office, might even take on a few local cases, pro bono." He shrugged.

Joy bubbled up from her belly, fizzling like champagne up her throat, and she bit the inside of her cheek to stifle a squeal. The emotions were too much, too overwhelming, and tears spilled over. She lowered her face, trying to hide them, which was futile with his gaze on her.

"Are those happy tears?" His baritone rasped across her senses, and she could do nothing but nod.

He clambered out of the booth, threw money onto the table, and she was airborne, tossed over his shoulder as he carried her out the diner. Applause and cries of encouragement accompanied their exit, and she clung to his back, fresh embarrassment burning her cheeks.

He flipped her to her feet beside his car, then pinned her to the door with his hips. Crowding her with his body and cupping her face forced her gaze to meet his.

Closing her eyes was the only way to escape that intensity crossing his features. "What have you done? My name will be on everyone's lips by lunchtime."

"What I have done is fallen in love with you, Amelia."

She flicked her eyes open on a gasp, tightening her fingers on his biceps. "What…did you say?" Maybe she *had* stepped through a portal. "It's the meds, right? I'm hallucinating." She giggled, tilting her head back to rest it against the car, scanning the blue sky in search of something to ground her.

"No, no drugs, just honesty. I love your stubborn ass, as much as I love your sensuality and creativity. I love your open heart, your compassion, as much as I adore the taste of your lips, the sweep of your tongue. I love your perfume. I love your sense of style …" He drew in a deep breath. "I *love* you, Amelia Perkins."

She studied his face, looking for a spark of humor. "You're serious?"

"Yes." He dipped his head to feather his lips across hers.

"I…uh…" She shuddered, and a sob tore from her now that reality had set in. "I love you too." She shook her head, tossing tears like a garden sprinkler. "I tried not to, to save myself. I tried so hard to resist, to be strong."

"Futile, right?" He grinned, exposing that one dimple that had a mainline to her heart. "It devastated me that you didn't return my calls, my texts, so I tried to move on, tried to return to my old ways. It didn't work." He pinched his lips. "None of the women interested me, and I couldn't orgasm without thinking of you, remembering you beneath me, in the bath, me buried in you." He smiled. "I became addicted to cherry soda in the hopes of capturing your flavor." He kissed her, sliding his tongue into her mouth on a groan. Wrapping his arms around her, he crushed her against him.

"It's too soon to ask you to marry me, but that's my goal," he whispered in her ear before nibbling on her lobe. "I'd like to date you, Amelia. I'd like you to move in with me, I want to wake up to you in my arms, and I want to fuck you on every surface in my new home."

She slid her hands along his shoulders to cup his jaw, kissing his chin. "Um…that's an intriguing offer, and a definite yes to all of it, Mr. Bradshaw."

He growled, snatching a hard kiss. "Call me Tom."

Epilogue

"MINDY, MOVE YOUR FAT head out of the way." Maude dared not blink when Tom took a willing Amelia into his arms. Mindy's trembling hands didn't help the situation while she filmed the couple from inside the diner. The screen shook so badly that nausea coiled in Maude's stomach, and a hint of a migraine pulsed behind her eyes. "Tom, don't be a dumbass." She was talking to herself, uncaring that Mindy could hear her through the video call.

"Our plan worked," Mindy cheered with the diner's patrons breaking into applause.

Maude wasn't going to concede to the likes of Mindy. She would never hear the end of it. "Our? Who had to pretend to faint then spend a night in the hospital?"

Mindy's face filled the screen, sidelining the kissing couple. "It was my cousin who played the doctor."

Maude snorted. "He *is* a doctor."

Mindy's smirk was arrogant and insufferable. "Exactly."

Maude huffed. "Fine... *Our* plan worked. I didn't raise a fool, Mindy. My dear Tom just needed a nudge." Her chest swelled with pride, shooting warmth to the tips of her toes. Damn, she loved that boy.

"When do you think they'll marry?" Mindy glanced at the couple.

"Who knows. They're both so stubborn. I'm not getting any younger, y'know. I want me some great grandbabies." Hell, if they had a long engagement, who knew when she could bounce a toddler on her knee, or even if her aging joints would allow it.

A wicked smile crawled across Mindy's face. "Fancy another trip to the hospital?"

Maude grinned, more than ready for another adventure. She wouldn't admit it to anyone, but the ambulance ride had been fun. "What do you have in mind?"

About the Author

Sevannah Storm is a fiction writer who immerses herself in fantastical worlds both magical and science fiction. She has a flare for the creative, having studied art and interior architecture, and spends her time drawing, oil painting, and writing. An avid reader from an early age, Sevannah finds her inspiration from various sources: games, novels, music, and the land of make-believe. The unique versus the practical has brought on numerous debates.

In her spare time, she does Pilates and rereads novels that snatch her breath away. Having embraced the social media world, you can find her on most platforms.

Her home is a land south of Wakanda, where animals roam free. Born in Zimbabwe, she grew up in South Africa. The crisp blue skies with cotton-candy sunsets expand her heart and soul, encapsulating a sense of freedom.

Words she lives by: "Know your pothole and dodge it. Don't work in a pencil factory if you're a vampire."

Sevannah loves to hear from her readers. You can find and connect with her at the links below.

Website/Newsletter:

https://www.sevannahstorm.com/

Facebook:

https://www.facebook.com/sevannah.storm

Instagram:

https://www.instagram.com/sevannah.storm/

Twitter:

https://twitter.com/sevannah_storm

Thank you for taking the time to read *Seducing Amelia*. If you enjoyed the story, please tell your friends and leave a review. Reviews support authors and ensure they continue to bring readers books to love and enjoy.